"When I look back now, I wonder how we would have felt if any of us had known that by the time summer was over at least two of us were going to suffer like we never had before, and none of us would ever be the same again."

For Camilla it was a time of learning about people, learning to accept them—and most of all, learning about herself. Camilla wrote it all down so she would never forget.

TRYING HARD TO HEAR YOU
by Sandra Scoppettone

TRYING HARD
TO HEAR YOU

Sandra Scoppettone

This low-priced Bantam Book
has been completely reset in a type face
designed for easy reading, and was printed
from new plates. It contains the complete
text of the original hard-cover edition.
NOT ONE WORD HAS BEEN OMITTED.

RLI: | VLM 3 (VLR 3–4)
IL 8+

TRYING HARD TO HEAR YOU
A Bantam Book / published by arrangement with
Harper & Row, Publishers

PRINTING HISTORY
Harper & Row edition published September 1974
2nd printing............August 1975
Bantam edition / August 1976
2nd printing

ISBN 0-553-02621-6

Published simultaneously in the United States and Canada.

Bantam Books are published by Bantam Books, Inc. Its trade-
mark, consisting of the words "Bantam Books" and the por-
trayal of a bantam, is registered in the United States Patent
Office and in other countries. Marca Registrada. Bantam
Books, Inc., 666 Fifth Avenue, New York, New York 10019.

PRINTED IN THE UNITED STATES OF AMERICA

Chapter 1

~~~~~~~~~~~~~~~~~~~~~~~~~~~~~~~~~~

You remember *Summer of '42*? You read the book? You at least saw the movie? Well, anyway it was kind of goony: It was all about when kids were nowhere and didn't have any ideas or music or terrific clothes or anything. And it was supposed to be this horrendous summer particularly for this one boy because he fell in love with this older woman and he had his poor little heart broken or something. Basically, it was a drag. And absolutely nothing compared to my summer of '73. Now that was a summer! I sound like it was years ago, don't I? Actually, this is only October of '73 and it's still very, very vivid, as you can imagine.

My friend Mary El's mother says that someday I won't even remember last summer or all the things that happened, or probably even the names of some of my friends. She says that someday if I hear the name Phil Chrystie I'll say: "Phil Chrystie? I think it sounds familiar but I can't quite place it." I find that hard to believe. But just in case she's right I've decided to write it all down so I'll never forget. Maybe some people would want to forget but not me. I like to remember everything that happens to me because someday when I'm a woman I can put everything together and see how I add up. Maybe that way I won't have to go lie on some analyst's couch like the people who come to see my mother.

I've always had a terrific memory. I even remember when I had whooping cough and I was only six months old. My mother says it's impossible for me to remember that but I know I do. If I close my eyes I can see the room, darkened except for an orange tulip-shaped light, and I can smell the musty odor of the inhalator and see my mother's white silky nightgown through the slats in my crib. My mother says I must have heard her and my father talking about it one time because it's impossible to remember anything from when you're six months old. She has very little faith. You can imagine that if she doesn't believe I remember that, she certainly doesn't believe that I flew when I was five.

I suppose you're thinking: who *is* this? Fly? She's really far out. Well, before you make any judgments listen to the facts. As I said, I was five. We were living in New Jersey at the time with my grandparents. They had a real old house with back stairs and pantries and stuff like that. Anyway, one rainy day my mother and my Aunt Kate were cleaning the downstairs. My aunt lived there too because her husband Bob was in the Vietnam War. It was in the afternoon, I remember, because I had had potato pancakes for lunch and I was feeling a little bit like I'd swallowed a couple of rocks. You see what I mean about my memory? How many people can remember what they ate for lunch eleven years ago?

So there I was, wandering around upstairs, peeking in everybody's drawers (something I wouldn't do today—I was very immoral when I was little), being real quiet so nobody would hear me and also so I wouldn't wake my baby sister Rachel who was taking a nap. There wasn't much doing in the drawers that day, no new stuff since I'd done my rounds the week before. Just the same old sachets in my grandma's drawers and no new photographs from my Uncle Bob in Aunt Kate's drawers and there was never anything interesting in my parents' drawers, so I decided to go downstairs and see if my mother would let me polish some silver. I guess most people wouldn't think polishing silver is any fun but it's something I've always liked doing. The blacker it is when I start the better I like it. I like the feeling of accomplishing something, seeing the silver shine, peering at my face all stretched out funny like when you look into a funhouse mirror. And it's good thinking time. These days I do a lot of important thinking when I shine silver. It's like when I chop vegetables for a salad or for my mother when she's going to make something Chinese in the wok. There's nothing like doing important thinking while you chop vegetables which, by the way, I get to do a lot more often than polishing silver.

When the silver polishing thing hit me I started down the first three steps of the red-carpeted staircase and stopped on the landing to listen. Kate and Mother were standing in the hall near the broom closet underneath the stairs. Kate was crying.

"Don't, Kate, you'll just make yourself sick," my mother said.

"I can't help it . . . I know it's crazy, but what if we get dragged into the war and he's involved in fighting? Oh, God, Laura, I'm so ashamed to admit this—I'm afraid he'll come back without a leg or an arm and I don't know if I could take that. I feel so guilty thinking that way."

"I'm sure we're not going to get dragged in but I understand your fear. You want the man you married. You wouldn't . . . or didn't . . . choose to marry someone who was crippled so why shouldn't you worry about that? I would. If Dan lost an arm or a leg I'm not sure I could handle it."

"Really?"

My mother said really and calmed Kate down and suggested they go on with the cleaning, and while they were standing there, right there next to the stairs, it happened. I flew down those stairs and landed at the bottom. Now don't go picturing me with my arms out flapping like a bird because that's not the way it happened. I stayed perpendicular to the

stairs but I was about six inches above them and I
just floated down. I don't know how I knew I could do
it or what made me try . . . it just happened. Suddenly, there I was floating down that staircase and landing
right next to Kate and my mother.

"Where'd you come from?" my mother said, whirling
around.

"I flew down the stairs," I said.

Well, there's no point in relating the whole dumb
dialogue between us because it ended the way it always did when I insisted on something that my mother considered a lie. Me in my room until dinner.

Those are just two examples of my fabulous memory. I could go on and on, like telling about my
memory of all the assassinations in the sixties and
depressing things like that but then you could say I
read about them or heard people talk about them and
it wouldn't prove a thing. The reason I'm so insistent
about this memory thing is that I want you to know
that what I'm going to tell you is absolutely true,
word for word—no embellishments . . . no coloring
. . . just plain, cold, hard facts . . . and a little emotion.

Here I've been rambling on about this thing and
that, and I haven't introduced myself. My mother says
my manners are atrocious and I guess she's right. My
name is Camilla (rhymes with vanilla) Crawford. I
am called: Cam, Cammy, and, sometimes, Camel. I
only allow my family and people I'm very close to to
call me Camel. I can't stand it when I'm introduced
to somebody new and right away they start calling
me Cam or Cammy. I think it's very nervy of people
to nickname you when they've just met you.

I was born on June 1, 1957. I'm a Gemini. The
Twins. I'm crazy about my birthday. I don't mean
having it every year, although I like that too. I
mean the date of it. I think the two nicest birthdates
in the year are September 1st and June 1st. They're

both the beginning of things. Even though officially June 21st is the beginning of summer I always think of the beginning of summer as June 1st. I also dig being a Gemini. It means I'm really two people in one . . . not like a schizophrenic with two distinct personalities, but just a person who has more options than other people. I mean, if you're two people then you have twice as many options. It stands to reason! Besides, I love what they say about Geminis in all those astrology books. Creative, volatile, intellectual, colorful, forceful, imaginative, and moody . . . which all adds up to being very interesting.

I suppose you're wondering if I'm all those things. Well, I am some of them and I think some of my friends would say that I'm pretty interesting. Even so, sometimes I think I'm the most boring person who ever lived. But, I have to admit, that's not too often.

I guess this would be as good a place as any to tell you that my father died when I was six. We had just moved into our own house in Maplewood, New Jersey, and the house was finally fixed up and Mother had planned a special dinner for Daddy and Rachel and me. It was a Friday night and we were all waiting around for Daddy to come home from work. Mother had martinis waiting in the refrigerator and I'd helped her set the table and arrange the flowers and pick which color candles. And then the phone rang. I remember that Mother got very white and she started to shake and when she hung up the phone she just stood there for a moment. Then she said that we'd have to go next door to stay with Mrs. Bishop, our neighbor. She said that Daddy was sick and she had to go to the hospital.

We stayed at the Bishops' all that night and in the morning Mother came to get us. She told us that Daddy had died. He'd had a heart attack. I remember that people were very shocked because Daddy was so young, and everybody cried a lot and made a big fuss over Rachel and me . . . but that's about all I remember. I guess I must have blocked it. Rachel and I didn't go to the funeral or anything because Mother said it wasn't right even though Daddy's parents had a big fight with her about it.

Mother sold the house in Maplewood after a few months and we moved to Seventh Avenue in New York, near Greenwich Village.

Now we live in Peconic, which is a small town between Southold and Cutchogue on the North Fork of Long Island. We actually live on Cedar Beach, on Peconic Bay. A lot of people have never heard of the North Fork, although more and more people are beginning to discover it every year, much to my mother's horror. Frankly I'm glad—the more the merrier. I can't understand why older people always want to isolate themselves.

We moved out here the summer of '67. Actually, we weren't planning to. We were just coming out for the summer like we always did and then, somewhere in the middle of the summer, Mother decided that it was a much better place to bring up kids and why didn't we just stay here permanently. Mother would go into the city three days a week to see her patients and if anybody wanted to see her out here they could see her in her study on Mondays or Fridays. So we went back to the city for a week, packed up everything, and moved out. Up until last year, when Mother was in the city Mrs. Horton stayed with us. I suppose she was a nice enough lady, but she had a habit of clicking her false teeth when she ate and it drove me crazy. It's a lot nicer without her . . . a lot quieter at mealtime.

Now sometimes on Tuesdays, Wednesdays, or Thursdays I sleep on the "shrink couch" in Mother's study because that room has the best view of the water. I love living on the water. I don't know how I ever survived without it. It makes me feel all peaceful when I'm uptight and anxious about something. I guess I'd call it soothing. Then sometimes in the winter when we have big storms the bay becomes really super wild . . . it almost looks like the ocean. Well, almost. And usually things are pretty dull in the winter, and watching it makes me feel all excited inside like when I feel I'm going to the dentist—only I know I'm not and so it's a nice feeling.

My best friend in the world is Jeff Grathwohl. He's a year and a half older than I am and he's in college this year and I don't mind saying that I miss him like crazy, even though we did get pretty far apart by the end of last summer. But I'm getting ahead of myself. Since Mother bought the house, Jeff and I have lived next door to each other. I mean our houses aren't on top of each other and yet I can see his house from my bedroom window in the winter when the leaves are off the trees. Jeff's an only child and Mr. and Mrs. Grathwohl are the most horrible parents a person could have. Jeff calls his father Affectionate Al, because he's about as affectionate as a rattlesnake, and I call his mother the Dragon Lady . . . but not to Jeff—he tends to like her.

In the summers Jeff and I had always played together and then when I moved out here permanently we became permanent friends. And nothing ever came between us or hurt our friendship in any way until last summer.

Jeff is very sophisticated for his age. He always has been. Maybe it's because he's always been a big reader. He says he's going to be a researcher. I'm not exactly sure I understand what that is or why anyone would pay you to do it but that's what he's going to be. As long as I've known him he's been researching one thing or another and he's always spouting these obscure statistics or theories that are fascinating but I really don't see how they'll add up to a career.

"Did you know that every day in this country fifteen thousand wild dogs are born?"

"No," I'd say.

"Well, it's true. What happens is that people get

dogs for pets in the summer and then, when the summer is over, they decide they don't want them. So they go back to the city, or wherever, and leave the dogs to fend for themselves. Then the dogs go off to the hills, or wherever, and they meet other dogs and start running in packs and mating and they multiply like crazy and so now fifteen thousand wild dogs are born every day."

"Fifteen thousand? A day?"

"Yes."

"I find that hard to believe, Jeff."

"It's true. I did research on it."

Or:

"Did you know that Picasso influenced almost every shape in the modern-day world?"

"What do you mean?"

"I mean if it wasn't for Picasso we wouldn't have the Kleenex box, for example."

"Picasso invented the Kleenex box?" I'd ask.

"He didn't invent it, dummy. He influenced its design. He wasn't an inventor, he was an artist."

"I know who he was. I just don't see how his painting has anything to do with the Kleenex box. I find that hard to believe."

"Well, it's true. I did research on it."

Our discussions of Jeff's statistics, or whatever they were, always ended that way. It never occurred to me to ask him where he did this research or to show me any proof. I just took what he said at face value except that often I did find it hard to believe.

Jeff is very handsome, if you like the type. He's tall and thin and has sort of chin-length blond hair and his eyes are very blue. Now although I could be friends with a blue-eyed person, I could never be romantically involved with one. It's very hard to know what a blue-eyed person is thinking . . . at least for me. Anyway, tons of girls felt very romantically about Jeff. They were always calling him up and making fools of themselves over him and though, over the years, he had one or two special girlfriends, he was always pretty cool about the droves who followed him around.

"You know who's a member of your fan club now?"

"Who?" he'd ask, his nose in a book, as cool as Alice Cooper being caught by the fuzz with an ounce of pot in his back pocket.

"Cindy Rimple, Robin Lytel, Debbie Fiedler, and Sharon Tuthill."

"Did you know that one out of every twelve drivers on the road is drunk?"

"Jeff, did you hear what I just said?"

"Yeah, I heard you."

"Well?"

"Well what?"

"Don't you care? I mean, Cindy and Robin and Debbie aren't much, but Sharon?"

Sharon Tuthill was just the most popular girl in her class, which was the year ahead of Jeff's.

"So what am I supposed to do? You want a handstand? Or maybe a double backflip?"

Jeff was a genius when it came to gymnastics. He'd won every prize there was to win by the time he graduated. People were always talking to him about going out for the Olympics next time around but he said he did it just for fun and didn't want to get that committed to something as unchallenging as gymnastics. My mother said Jeff didn't want to pursue it because he'd rather be a big fish in a little pond.

"Don't you think Sharon is cute?"

"Sure."

"Well?"

"Well what, for God's sake?"

"Aren't you going to ask her out or anything?"

"Maybe. I'll see."

But he never did. In fact, he never asked any of the girls out who were in his fan club. The summer

before last he dated Tina Heacock all through Youth
On Stage but when the show was over he stopped
seeing her. By the way, Youth on Stage is just what
it sounds like . . . a group of kids, sometimes as many
as sixty or seventy, who get together and put on a
musical at the North Fork Community Theater during
the summer.

I don't mind telling you that I envied Jeff. Normally I'm not an envious person but I couldn't help wishing it was me who had tons of boys chasing me. And
I wouldn't have been the least put out if there had
been a Camilla Crawford fan club. Now I don't want
you to get the idea that I'm ugly or that I've never
had a date or anything because that just isn't true.
I've never been a Sharon Tuthill but I've had my
share of boyfriends. Well, I guess that's stretching the
truth a little unless you call "my share" two. There
was George Wilks in the ninth grade and last year,
for two months, there was Harlan Young. George was
almost a head shorter than I was which wouldn't have
been the end of the world but on top of that I don't
think he ever took a bath. People were always calling him "Pigpen" behind his back, like the character
in *Peanuts*, and it was beginning to ruin my reputa-
tion. Besides, I almost threw up every time he came
close to me. I thought a lot about telling him the
truth or just handing him a bar of soap but I just
couldn't bring myself to do it. My mother said he
probably let himself smell that way to get attention.
Whatever the reason was he got over it, because this
summer I never saw anybody so clean. But once something is over it's over and I could never go back to
George.

Harlan Young was another story. He was clean and
neat and a head taller than I but after a while I just
couldn't tolerate his values. All he ever thought about
was money. He's going to be an orthodontist because
they make lots of money, even though he thinks it's
one of the most boring things you could be. I just

can't see doing something to make money. I mean, I'd rather be starving and do something I like. But not Harlan. He said that his father always taught him the value of a dollar and he's grateful for it. You won't believe this but when Harlan was a little boy and his father gave him fifty cents a week allowance, he actually only got forty-five cents because his father kept five for taxes. He said his father did it to teach him what it would be like when he started earning money of his own. Frankly, I think it's because his father is cheap. Anyway, Harlan is very intelligent and good-looking in an odd sort of way—not your typical all-American type, by any means—but his thing with money finally drove me up the wall. He was always into money-making schemes like charging people to ride on his bicycle or taping albums and selling them for a dollar cheaper than the stores. Actually, those weren't too bad, but when I learned about the baby thing, that was the last straw.

We have in Greenport a kind of black ghetto. I don't know why I say kind of. It is. It's better known as Cardboard City and, though people like my mother and the Larsens (when they used to live here) and the Feinbergs keep bringing it up at town meetings, they have a lot of opposition and nothing ever seems to happen. By the way, Greenport is one of the larger towns around and is also a boat harbor. It's near the end of the Fork between Southold and East Marion. I don't know how the whole thing started with Harlan or how he got the idea but he had been doing it about two years before he told me. He would find out about a black woman who was pregnant and go and visit her and tell her that he could predict whether she was going to have a boy or a girl and for five dollars he'd be glad to tell her and if he was wrong he'd cheerfully refund her money. Well, even if he was right only one out of ten he was still ahead of the game and, of course, being Harlan, he was right more than fifty percent of the time. He'd never told anyone about it until he told me.

"You're kidding," I said.

"Nope. Neat, isn't it?"

"I think it's disgusting."

He was shocked. "Why?"

"Because it's immoral. You're taking advantage of those poor women. Ripping them off."

"No I'm not. I give them their money back if I'm wrong."

"But, Harlan, you're just guessing."

"So what? They don't know that. It makes them happy."

"But anybody could tell them that."

"Yeah, but I thought of it," he said, grinning.

Well, nothing I said made the slightest difference to him. He had an answer for every argument I gave him. Before he told me I had promised I wouldn't tell anyone so there was nothing I could do about it except not see him anymore and that's what I did. It's hard for me to believe that Harlan is going to be happy being an orthodontist. Even though he probably will make a lot of money, it's honest work and somehow I can't believe that will really appeal to him.

So those were my two main boyfriends. I had other dates here and there but no one amounted to anything . . . until last summer when I remet Phil Chrystie. Phil had been in *South Pacific* the summer before playing Lieutenant Cable and I had been in the chorus and I used to see him all the time, but he really didn't pay too much attention to me. In fact, I don't think he knew I was alive because that summer he only had eyes for Kitty Larsen. In the fall he went away to college and I didn't see him again until this past summer's tryouts for *Anything Goes*, the show Youth On Stage was going to do.

The tryouts were on June twenty-third and twenty-fourth and our whole crowd was there, plus lots of other kids. We were all high on the prospect of doing the show but, when I look back now, I wonder how we would have felt if any of us had known that by the time the show was over at least two of us were going to suffer like we never had before, one of us would almost be tarred and feathered, two of us would be dead, and none of us would ever be the same again.

Chapter 2

I guess what I should do now is tell you a little bit about our crowd. I've already told you something about Jeff and, believe me, it's just a smattering because Jeff is a very complex person. Anyway, his personality will unfold as I go along. I'm going to be very honest . . . very upfront about us. We're *not* the *in* crowd. What I mean by that is that we're not the cheerleaders and the jocks (except for Jeff) or the most popular or the prettiest or the most handsome (except for Jeff) or the fashion leaders or any of that stuff. What we are is a group of people who read and have outside interests and most us love acting or painting or something artistic. And I don't mind telling you that most of us are pretty smart. Did you ever notice that the smart kids are rarely the *in* group? My mother says that the kids who are the most popular in school usually grow up to be the dullest. I hope she's right. Now I'm not saying that our group consists of a bunch of misfits, although I suppose the *in* group might look at us that way. Actually, I don't see how you can be misfits in a group. If you belong to a group or you're in a crowd of any sort then you fit that crowd and, therefore, you can't be a misfit. That's just logical. I suppose what you could say about us is that we're different. Interesting.

At the start of the summer of '73 the nucleus of our group consisted of seven kids. There were Jeff and me

and Walt Feinberg, Janet Clark, Sam Ahlers, Mary
El Merensky, and Penny Lademan. Tina Heacock was
part of the group depending on who she was going
with. Tina didn't like girls her own age so we never
knew too much about her except that she has this
sensational singing voice. The summer before last, as
I said, she was going with Jeff so she was pretty much
part of the nucleus, and as we started the summer of
'73 she was going with Walt so once again she was
with us.

Walt is the brain of all of us. He was the valedic-
torian of his graduating class this year and he's going
to go into political science. A lot of kids think Walt
is a show-off in terms of his braininess and then there
are some kids who simply think he's a pain in the
ass, but I know that basically he's a very insecure
person and, like everyone else, all he needs is love.
I think one of his main problems is that his grandfather, who owns Feinberg's Department Store in
Southold, was a friend of Albert Einstein's and everybody is always talking about that and making a big
deal of it and Walt's grandfather is always being
written up in the *Times* or someplace as this big
friend of Einstein's, who, incidentally, used to spend
his summers out here. I think maybe Walt has an
inferiority complex and wants to grow up to be more
important than Einstein or something. My mother
says I make too much out of the Einstein thing and
that Walt comes from a very intellectual family and
it's just a simple matter of competition with his father.
But I say no. I mean, if my grandfather had been a
good friend of Bette Davis's and everybody was always writing about that, I'd certainly feel inferior as
an actress. The other thing about Walt is that he says
whatever he feels like saying no matter where he is
or who he's with and that drives a lot of kids up the
wall. Like last year at Janet Clark's sixteenth birthday party. We were all sitting around enjoying ourselves and Walt looked over at Sam who was sitting
in his usual manner, one leg crossed over the other at

a forty-five degree angle and jiggling the crossed leg
a mile a minute.

"You know why you jiggle your leg like that, Sam?"

"It's a nervous habit."

"Yeah, it's that all right, but there's another reason."

"Well, please, don't keep us in suspense," Sam said.
He's very sarcastic when he wants to be.

"It's because you masturbate a lot."

Well, you can imagine the reaction that got. Sam
said that was a lie and Janet said Walt had no right
to say things like that and Walt said it was a free
country and Tina said Walt was just showing off and
Penny couldn't stop giggling and Mary El blushed and
I tried to change the subject and Jeff said:

"Did you know that a man named Charles Hamilton, alias Frank Richard, wrote 72 million words in
his lifetime?"

"So what?" Walt said.

"So that's incredible, that's what."

"What did he write?" I asked, hoping everyone
would get interested.

"Comics," Jeff said.

The discussion of Charles Hamilton ended there and
nobody could think of anything to say, which is unusual with our group, and about ten minutes after
Walt's little pronouncement we all went home. Anyway, that is the kind of thing Walt will say.

Janet is kind of the mother of us all. Everybody
goes to her with problems. Maybe that's why she's going to be a guidance counsellor. She's very smart and
she listens like crazy. That's a real art in itself. I know
I have trouble listening. I try because I know that you
can't learn anything if you don't listen but I always
seem to have so much to say. But Janet can listen for
hours. Not that she doesn't talk . . . she does. But
she's basically a listener. The thing about Janet is that
she's overweight—fat. She's always been fat, according to her.

"When I was in the fifth grade I weighed two hundred pounds. They had to get a special desk and chair for me. I don't remember feeling embarrassed. I just remember feeling special."

Frankly, I think she's blocked her embarrassment. The summer before last she was the only one of our crowd who got to know Phil Chrystie and she fell in love with him. Janet is always falling in love with impossible people. Before Phil it was Mr. Rickers, the school principal. Whenever we mention this little hangup to her she says that, in her case, everyone is impossible so what difference does it make? I guess she has a point. Anyway, she wrote to Phil at college this year and in February she decided to go on a diet. By the time Phil came home from college she had lost forty-three pounds.

"Did he say anything about your weight loss?" I asked after she had spent an afternoon with him.

"When you look like me," she said, "forty-three pounds is like a weight loss of a pound from an elephant."

She's very philosophical. And sensible. She's not doing any crash diet stuff, she's just eating like a normal person now. I was very afraid when everything happened that she'd go back to eating like a pig again, but she started to smoke instead and, in her case, that was much healthier.

Sam Ahlers is an artist . . . and a puppeteer. Last year he made all the puppets for the NFCT, North Fork Community Theater, that is, production of *Carnival.* Everyone said they were wonderful. And he did the makeup and some of the costumes. Now here is a perfect example of why our group is our group. We think Sam is terrific. We admire his talent. We encourage him. The *in* group would think he was fruity. They'd put him down and say terrible nasty things about him and make him feel like an outcast. But not us. When he moved here the summer before last we took him right into our group because we were happy to have somebody so talented and clever be part of us. Besides, Sam is very cute—particularly since he grew his mustache. There's only one thing about Sam that bothers me. He's very self-involved. All he can think about are his own problems. This is a typical conversation with Sam:

> ME: Have you noticed that Janet seems a little depressed?
>
> SAM: She doesn't know what depressed is. She should try living with my father. Then she'd know what depressed is.
>
> ME: I don't think I've seen her laugh for days.
>
> SAM: You want to know a laugh that could drive you crazy? My mother laughs like a hyena. Sometimes when she starts laughing I think I could strangle her.
>
> ME: Maybe we should try and do something to cheer her up.
>
> SAM: My mother? Why? She's cheerful enough. That's the whole point . . . she's always laughing. Aren't you listening?

Sam's self-involvement is a definite failing, but he's kind and I guess his talent makes up for everything. At least it does for Mary El Merensky, who is madly in love with him. Mary El is my best girlfriend . . . well, actually, both she and Janet are. They fulfill different needs for me. Janet is my mother confessor or something and Mary El is more of a buddy. Mary El is always ready to do something crazy with me. Like the time we organized our whole geometry class to belch in tune to "London Bridge" every time this creepy substitute teacher turned her back to do some awful equation on the board. There was nothing she could do about it either because we had it arranged so that the different belches came from every point in the room and I guess the teacher felt she couldn't send a whole class to detention or it would make her look incompetent. So instead, she just sat

down at her desk and started to cry. Mary El and
I felt awful then but there was nothing we could do
about it at that point except to try and keep the other
kids from laughing. We didn't have much success with
that. It's a lot easier to get kids to do something rotten than to do something nice.

Anyway, Mary El will do almost anything and
that's what I like best about her. She's willing to take
chances with life. But she's madly in love with Sam,
who is madly in love with this older woman, Linda,
who is a senior in college and a friend of Sam's
family. No, it's not like *Summer of '42* because the
woman is happily engaged and just thinks Sam's a
nice kid. Sam is seeing an analyst about it. My mother
says that that's why Sam's so self-involved. She says
many people get very self-involved when they're first
in analysis. Sam's parents think he's seeing an analyst
because he doesn't get along with them, which is
partially true, I guess. Mary El is always hanging
on Sam and even though I try and tell her to keep it
cool, she can't seem to control her emotions. Naturally, Sam knows how Mary El feels and he's told her
all about Linda, but, Mary El feels that eventually
he'll get over Linda and turn to her.

One of the biggest problems Mary El has is her
mother. The moment she brings a boy into the house
her mother looks at him like a prospective husband.
Really. When she was fourteen and brought home
Andy Maher, who was thirteen and there just to
work on a science project, Mrs. Merensky started
right in.

"Oh, what a nice couple you make. Look . . . look
in the mirror and see how good you look together."

"Mama, please," Mary El said, "Andy's just a
friend."

"Oh, the burdens I carry . . . the burdens I carry."

That's one of Mrs. Merensky's favorite lines. The
moment you disagree with her she starts in about her
burdens. We refer to her as the Mammoth Martyr because she's rather large and the martyr part is self-

explanatory. We also love alliteration! As you can imagine, Mary El hates to bring boys into the house. The only reason we can see for the Mammoth Martyr's behavior is that she didn't get married until *she* was thirty-four and is afraid Mary El will end up the same way, a fate worse than death as far as she's concerned. Mary El's father still speaks with a heavy accent and mostly he says, "I'm strong as bull."

The Mammoth Martyr said recently if the Bull doesn't start listening to her, she's going to have him committed. Frankly, I think the only way the Bull keeps sane is by *not* listening to her. Mary El wants to be a physical therapist.

What can I say about Penny Lademan? Crazy, I think. Well, not really . . . not like crazy-truly-insane, but more like crazy-manic. I never knew anyone who had more energy than Penny. She was always bouncing around and making faces and dancing and singing and doing a million things. She was a good actress and a good singer and in tenth grade she had the lead in *Once Upon A Mattress*. At least she had it for three weeks. Then she and a bunch of kids she used to hang out with sometimes cut school and went over to Ralph Laine's, whose parents were in the Bahamas, and they all got drunk and ended up on the beach screaming and throwing each other in the bay. It was February and some lady called the police and, naturally, they were all caught and Mr. Safier took the part away from Penny. Well, she changed a bit after that. I mean, she didn't do any more self-destructive things but she still stayed crazy. For instance, it didn't surprise anyone to see Penny coming down the hall wearing her raincoat backward and a bathing cap on her head. She was always doing things like that. Or walking around a whole day with her left shoe on her right foot and her right shoe on her left foot and pretending nothing's wrong. Did you ever see Dondi in the funny papers? Well, that's what Penny looked like. Great big round black eyes, a tiny nose, and a sweet little mouth in a round face with straight black hair and bangs. Anyway, when we arrived at the theater for auditions we were all positive that Penny would get the lead.

Chapter 3

~~~~~~~~~~~~~~~~~~~~~~~~~~~~~~~~~~

The night before tryouts we were all in Fisherman's Rest having a pizza. The main topic of conversation was Youth On Stage and what it would be like to work with Susan Stimpson who was taking over for Mrs. Larsen who had started YOS two years before but had to move away this past January. None of us really knew Stimpson except Janet, who had worked with her on *Who's Afraid of Virginia Woolf?* for the NFCT.

"Now listen, don't act like I'm some big authority on her or something. I don't know much about her either. All I did was stage manage for her . . . we never got into any personal conversations or anything."

"I hear she's a big drinker."

"Oh, Walt," everybody said.

"Well, I'm sorry, but that's what I heard."

Tina rolled her eyes back in her head which is what she always did when Walt said something that embarrassed or irritated her. Lately, she was looking like she had two white stones for eyes almost all the time.

"There was this guy in England named Vanhorn who drank 35,688 bottles of ruby port in twenty-three years," Jeff said.

"I once drank all the dregs from the glasses at a party my parents gave," Sam said. "Oh, God, did I get sick. I was four."

Walt took a big swallow of Coke, cleared his throat, straightened his round steel-rimmed glasses, and sitting back in his chair, looking as though he'd just been invited to a Stones concert in *his* honor, he said, "That would be four bottles a day."

"No," Sam said, "*I* was four—what are you talking about bottles for? I said I drank the . . ."

"I'm talking about the guy in England."

Then suddenly Penny gave one of her famous screams. I guess you could say it was a cross between a kung-fu yell and a Siamese cat in heat, if you can imagine that. We all jumped and so did everyone else in the place. There was dead silence and then a waitress came running over.

"Okay . . . okay, that's it . . . you kids get your tails out of here. What do you think this is, the school gym or somethin'?"

"We have not finished our repast, Madam," Walt said, holding a slice of pizza over his mouth like a sword swallower.

"I don't care if you haven't finished the repast *or* the pizza," she said, both her hands on her hips. "Pay up and get out. This is a respectable place and we don't want no screamin' banshees around here."

"Look, lady," Penny said, "if you'll just hold your horses I can explain."

"Out."

Penny went on. "The reason I screamed was because the most repulsive and the biggest bug I've ever seen was in my Coke. I mean, what would you do?"

The waitress eyed her for a moment and then she crossed her bony arms in front of her, threw one of her hips to the side, and very slowly said, "Show me."

"I can't," Penny said.

"Oh yeah? Why not?"

"Because I swallowed it."

Well, naturally she blew the whole thing when she said that so we had to pay and get out.

We all piled into Walt's '62 Dodge Dart (called the Silver Bullet) and drove over to Kenny's Beach and parked. It was still pretty early in the season and there was a kind of chill in the air but with three of us stuffed in the front and five in the back we didn't notice.

"Why the hell *did* you scream?" Jeff asked.

"Because we weren't getting anywhere. I told you, I need to know how to behave with this Stimpson character."

"I don't see what difference it makes how you come on, Pen," Janet said. "What matters is your audition."

"Well, I thought maybe I could butter her up or something if I knew a little bit about her. I wish Mrs. Larsen were doing it."

"Are you kidding?" Sam said. "Then you really wouldn't have a chance."

Helen Larsen had cast her daughters as leads in each of the shows she'd done, even though there had been better people for the parts. And if she'd done the show this year there was no doubt in my mind that Betty Larsen would have gotten the lead. She was the next daughter in line, and there were four daughters after that.

"If you mean Betty, I don't think Mrs. Larsen would have cast her . . . she's too young. Besides, Mrs. Larsen liked me."

"What's the difference what *would* have happened," Jeff said. "Stop living in the past. Stimpson is the one you have to worry about now."

"Anyway, Pen, I'm going to be on the casting committee."

Janet was going to be the producer. The only adults involved in YOS are the director, the musical director, and the choreographer. Everything else is done by the kids.

"Who else will be on the committee?" Penny asked, her Dondi eyes reflecting the light of the flame from Jeff's lighter. Jeff was starting his second pack of Marlboros today and it worried me. He was smoking more and more lately.

"Me, Stimpson, Etta Smith, for advice, and Phil Chrystie."

"Phil Chrystie?" Everyone said it at once.

Janet smiled her smile which almost closed her eyes.

"I bet I can't guess whose idea that was," I said.

"As a matter of fact, Cam, I had nothing to do with it. Phil called up Stimpson himself and asked if he could be her assistant."

"You mean," Walt said, running a hand through his black curly hair, "old stiff Lt. Cable isn't trying out for the show?"

"Oh, Walt," Tina said, "that's mean."

"Well, hell, he *was* stiff."

"That's because his father told him lieutenants are very stiff," Janet said defensively. "Anyway, he knows he's a rotten actor and that's why he wanted to be assistant director."

"He sure does have a beautiful voice though," I said, remembering how I used to stand backstage, my eyes closed, listening to him sing "Younger Than Springtime" and wishing he were singing it to me.

"He still stinks as an actor."

"Oh, Walt."

"Who else is on the committee?" Penny asked.

"That's all."

Mary El said: "Well then, I don't see what you have to worry about, Penny. You have it made."

"Except for one thing," Jeff said, practically hidden behind a cloud of smoke.

"What's that?"

"Maura Harris?"

"What about her?"

"She's trying out. I heard some kids talking about it in Greenport the other day."

"Panic grips my heart," Penny said, clutching her chest and crossing her eyes.

"I happen to know," Janet said in her best mother-of-us-all voice, "that before she left, Mrs. Larsen warned Stimpson about Maura. I don't think she'd give Maura the part if she was the last one on earth."

"What'd Mrs. Larsen say about her?" I asked.

"She told her that Maura drinks a lot and she's trouble."

"Gross," Mary El said. "Mrs. Larsen never liked Maura ... probably because she knew she should have had the lead in *South Pacific* instead of her fat daughter. Maura was much better than Peggy."

Penny was starting to sink down to the floor.

"Oh, she's not that good," I said.

"She's too short."

"She can't see without her glasses."

"Did ya ever dig that nose? Now that's a nose."

"How about her lisp?"

"And her buck teeth."

"And that stupid giggle."

"She's nowhere as good as you, Pen," Janet said. "You've as good as got the part right now."

"You think so?"

We all agreed except Jeff, who hung his head out the window as he lit up another Marlboro.

"You've got it made," Walt said. "Let's celebrate." He opened his glove compartment. "I just happen to have a brand-new fresh bottle of Boone's Farm Strawberry Hill Wine."

We passed the bottle around (it really was disgusting stuff) and by the time we finished we were all calling Penny Reno Sweeney, which is the name of the lead in *Anything Goes*.

When Walt dropped Jeff and me off I was feeling a little dizzy from the wine so I hung onto Jeff's arm as we walked down the path to my house. Suddenly he stopped.

"I think what you all did was stupid," he said.

"What?"

"You shouldn't have gotten Penny so excited about the part. What if she doesn't get it?"

"But she will."

"You don't know that, Cam. Maura Harris is very good whether any of you will admit it or not. She's damn good, in fact. You saw her in *Hello, Dolly!*, for God's sake."

"I thought she was awful."

"You're just jealous. You all are and you make me puke." He pulled away from me and ran across the road toward his house.

I watched him go, his outline fading into the darkness. What was that all about, I wondered. Then all of a sudden it occurred to me that maybe Jeff dug Maura. Jeff and Maura! I hated the idea. Nothing could be worse. Little did I know that something could be . . . and would be.

Chapter 4

~~~~~~~~~~~~~~~~~~~~~~~~~~~~~~~~~

The theater is in Mattituck. Actually, it was once a church and from the outside it still looks a lot like a church. To the left of the building, as you face it, is a cemetery. A lot of the kids make out or drink beer in there but, frankly, cemeteries never did appeal to me. On the big white board against the gray of the theater, the sign said:

YOUTH ON STAGE

Tryouts for
ANYTHIN GOES
JUNE 23 & 24

I found out later that they couldn't find a third G. When Jeff and Mary El and Sam and I arrived, there were about ten kids sitting outside on the steps. We knew all of them and were pretty sure none of them would be trying out for leads, so we smiled and exchanged greetings. Inside, there were only about four kids and Janet.

"Here's an application. Fill it out and if you're trying out for a lead give it to Miss Stimpson."

"Aren't we formal," I said.

"Beat it," she said, smiling.

"Where is everybody?" Jeff asked.

"I think most of the kids have gone to the Strawberry Festival."

"You know why strawberries are called *straw*berries?" Jeff asked.

"Why?"

"Well, there are quite a few theories. First of all..."

"Never mind," I said, dragging him out of Janet's way. Four other kids were lined up behind us waiting for their applications.

As Jeff and I walked to the middle of the theater to take our seats I kept peering around to see if Maura Harris was there. She was probably creepy enough to go to the Strawberry Festival.

I guess you're wondering what this Strawberry Festival is. Well, here on the North Fork we grow a lot of strawberries, and once a year, on the grounds of the Mattituck High School, they have this Festival. What it consists of are a few booths where you can pitch pennies or rings or throw darts for crummy plaster statue prizes, a few antiques and artists' displays, and, of course, the big tent where, for a dollar and a half, you can make a pig of yourself hogging down all the strawberry shortcake you can eat. Last year Billy Witherspoon ate thirty pieces and then puked all over himself. It was disgusting. But the really big event of the day is the arrival, by helicopter, of the Strawberry Queen and her Court. To me that is even more disgusting than Billy Witherspoon throwing up all over himself. I mean, let's face it: the Strawberry Queen, the Firehouse Queen, the Sea Bass Queen, the Queen of the Prom, and all the other four million queens we seem to have around here are nothing but sex objects. I think it's really creepy to have these contests for the prettiest this or the prettiest that. I know you think it's because I never could win and I'm jealous or something but really it's not. I just happen to be interested in Women's Lib and I realize that those kinds of contests are sexist and degrading to women and, besides that, they're boring. Anyway, anyone who would go to the Strawberry Festival, if they've ever been once, has to be a real creep and since Maura Harris has lived here for the last two years I'm sure she's gone before so I thought it was very creepy of her to have gone again and I said so to Jeff.

"How do you know that's where she is?"

"I just have a feeling. It's the kind of thing she'd do."

"Camilla," he said, his blue eyes boring into mine, "you don't even know her so how can you know the kind of thing she'd do or not do? The answer is, you *can't*. So fill out your application and shut up."

He turned back to his application and once again I wondered why he was so intent on defending Maura. I decided to ask him later when he wasn't quite so tense. Jeff isn't the best actor in the world and he always got very cranky when he was about to audition. I waved to Penny, Tina, and Walt who had just come in and then settled down to filling out my application. This is what it looked like:

YOUTH ON STAGE—SUMMER 1973

The show will be ANYTHING GOES
Performances 4 to 8
                    Definite Dates August 10, 11, 17, 18

Rehearsals will begin on June 25th.
We will rehearse Mondays through Fridays from 7:30 to 10:00 P.M.

If you would like to be onstage or in the backstage crew please fill out this form

Name_____ Phone No._____
Age___ Grade in school_____ School_____
Were you in MUSIC MAN? _____
Onstage _____ Backstage _____
Were you in SOUTH PACIFIC? _____
Onstage _____ Backstage _____
Have you had lessons in singing? _____

Voice Range _____
Tenor_____ Baritone_____ Alto_____ Soprano_____
Will you sing solo?_____ Chorus?_____
Have you had lessons in dance?_____
Can you tap dance?_____
Are you interested in a speaking part?_____
A lead?_____
Have you had any other experience?_____
Parts played_____
If not needed onstage will you work
      backstage?_____ or on a committee?_____
If yes, check jobs interested in:
      Building sets___ Makeup___
      Publicity___ Ushers___
      Painting sets___ Stage Manager___
      Props___ Stage Crew___ Tickets___
      Program___ Costumes___
      Lights and Sound___ House Manager___

If you join this project certain things will be re-
quired of you. You will be responsible for your scripts
and if lost or damaged you will be charged the Tams-
Witmark price. If you miss more than four rehearsals
without a legitimate excuse you will be dropped
from the show. If you are not scheduled for a rehearsal you will not be permitted in the theater or on
the grounds. Anyone found smoking marijuana or
drinking alcoholic beverages on the NFCT premises
will be dropped from the show. Remember: The ob-
ject of this project is to have fun. Don't spoil it!

I read the last paragraph twice. Smoking marijuana!
I assumed Stimpson had written the application and
I wondered just what kind of person she was. Even
Mrs. Merensky called it pot. I suppose she decided
if she said pot she would be getting down to our
level and by saying marijuana she would remain an
authority figure. I know a lot about authority figures
from my mother. The thing I liked best about that
paragraph was the part about the alcoholic beverages

because if, by some crazy chance, Maura got the part she'd be sure to drink and get kicked out.

I filled out the application saying I wanted a speaking part, a lead, that I would sing solo (my voice is just passable), and that if I didn't get a part I would stage manage or work on sets, publicity, or lights. Of course, I had my heart set on a part. From what Janet had told me about the show there was a good part for me, the part of Bonnie, a gangster's moll who's kind of crazy. I could never play an ingenue or something serious. I like to play crazy characters because I can really hide behind them. I mean it's much more pretend that way and that's what acting is all about, isn't it? I looked around the theater and saw Stimpson sitting in the back. She was talking with Sam. I walked over and gave her my application. She smiled and thanked me. Then I went back and sat down next to Jeff, who was still filling out his application. Finally he finished and, without a word to me, took it back to Stimpson. Then he came back and sat down.

"I'll probably end up in the chorus like last year," he said.

"Don't be so negative."

"Well, let's face it, I can't really sing . . . or dance . . . or act."

"You can sing okay, and your acting isn't half bad."

"Thanks," he said sarcastically.

I was about to go into a big long thing about how good he was in the chorus of *South Pacific* and how he stood out (which he did because he was always on his left foot when everyone else was on their right) when I looked up and saw Phil Christie coming through the door.

Now I know this is going to sound dramatic or adolescent or corny, but when I saw him my heart skipped a beat. It really did. I felt it. Not to mention what happened to my stomach. Also I felt myself blushing which is the last thing in the world I wanted to happen. I once read that people blush to attract attention to themselves but I can't believe that's true because whenever I blush I wish I was invisible and the last thing I want is for anyone to notice me. Of course, they always do.

"What's the matter with you? You're red as a beet," Jeff said.

"Nothing," I said quickly and looked down at my feet.

"What do you mean, nothing? Either something happened and you're blushing or you just made the world's record for the most sudden fever."

"I don't know what you're talking about."

"Come on, Camel, what's up?"

"Nothing. Really." I just couldn't explain to him. Not that he would have laughed at me or anything— Jeff never laughed at people's emotions—but I felt foolish having that kind of reaction to someone I barely knew. "Let's drop it, okay?"

"Something did happen then, right?"

"Yes, but I . . ." Just then, thank God, I heard my name called. It was Stimpson. "I'll tell you later," I said and quickly left my seat and walked back to where she was sitting.

I sat down next to her and tried to concentrate on the interview, putting Phil Christie out of my mind for the moment.

"Why do you want to be in this show, Camilla?" she was saying.

"Well, I love to act. In fact, I want to be an actress someday."

"Really? I see by your application you've done a bit of it in school."

I had played Mrs. Stanley in *The Man Who Came to Dinner*, Mrs. Savage in *The Curious Savage*, and Agnes Gooch in *Auntie Mame*.

"I also see that you're worried about your singing."

On the back of the application I had written: "My voice is not terribly good. I would appreciate it if more attention was paid to my readings. Thank you."

"Well, I suppose you know that all of the large

speaking parts require singing. What part were you thinking of trying out for?"

"Bonnie."

"She has two big numbers, Camilla."

"Yes, I know that. I didn't mean I couldn't sing at all; I just meant that I'm a better actress than singer."

"You *are* prepared to sing something for me, aren't you?"

"Yes."

"Good. Okay, thanks for talking with me. I'll see you later."

I thanked her and walked back to my seat. Jeff wasn't there. About thirty kids were in the theater now. My sister Rachel was one of them. Last year she had been too young for YOS but now that she was fourteen she was eligible. She was planning to try out for the chorus and I was sure she would make it because she had a really neat voice. I just hoped she wouldn't try hanging around me all summer. I really didn't need that.

"All ready for the euthanasia tryouts?"

It was Walt taking a seat behind me. He always called Youth On Stage euthanasia.

"Ready as I'll ever be," I said.

Just then a whistle blew and Miss Stimpson said she'd like to hear Sam Ahlers sing. I was awfully glad I wasn't first. Sam walked over to the piano, gave Alan Kates his music, and went up on stage. Everybody was very quiet and just as Sam started to sing the "Soliloquy" from *Carousel*, Phil Chrystie sat down beside me. I thought I was going to pass out.

Chapter 5

I don't know if he looked at me or not when he sat down because I didn't dare look at him. I could feel myself starting to blush again and right away I could feel my blouse starting to stick to me. Sam was singing on and on and Phil was sitting so close I could feel him breathing. Finally the song was over and everybody started clapping. I guess I clapped louder and longer than anybody just out of sheer nervousness.

"Okay, Sam, thank you. From now on, people, let's not have any applause," Stimpson said. "May I hear Tina Heacock, please."

As Tina walked over to the piano I felt Phil's eyes on me. I knew I couldn't ignore him forever, so slowly I turned to face him. He was smiling, his brown eyes looking directly into mine. He had grown a mustache for the part of Lt. Cable the summer before and he had kept it. The shock of brown hair that he had had to spray when he was on stage to keep it from falling in his eyes was loose now and touched the top of one eyebrow.

"Hi," he said, "remember me?"

"Sure," I said, trying to sound as casual as possible.

"You look different."

"I'm just the same except a year older."

"Maybe that's it," he said, smiling gently; "I guess you look more mature."

"Really?"

He nodded as the piano began the intro for "Bali Ha'i," the song Tina was going to sing. Mature. No one had ever said that about me before. Was it possible that Phil was going to pay attention to *me* this year? And maybe I hadn't gone as unnoticed last year as I thought. Maybe he was just waiting for me to turn sixteen and become more *mature*. Tina's voice was filling the theater and Phil's presence and what he'd said were filling *me*. The song was over and as I started to applaud Phil grabbed my hands and shook his head. He'd touched me! But I felt foolish because it was as though I was a child and he was the parent telling me what to do. The foolishness went away quickly when I realized he was holding onto my hands a little bit longer than he had to. Then Stimpson called his name to come and help her with something and he let go of my hands, stood up, and leaned over to me.

"Good luck, Brenda," he whispered, and was off down the aisle.

BRENDA? Who was Brenda? The only Brenda I knew was Tina Heacock's fourteen-year-sister who hadn't even been around during *South Pacific*. Brenda? Was Brenda someone he'd met at college? A lost love? Someone who had hurt him dreadfully? Would he forever be calling all girls Brenda? But more important, could I be the one to make him forget Brenda?

"What were you talking to that fink about?" Jeff asked, sitting down where Phil had been.

"What fink?"

"Chrystie."

"Oh, nothing much. Why is he a fink?"

"I don't know . . . there's just something about him I don't like. He's too smooth or something."

"He's just very gentle."

"Oh, is that what he is?" Jeff said, sarcastically. He slipped down in his seat and put his legs over the chair in front of him. I couldn't help thinking that Jeff was acting very peculiar lately but I was much too involved with thinking about Phil to spend too much time on Jeff.

The auditions continued and even though Stimpson had asked us not to applaud everyone cheered after Penny sang the title song from *Cabaret*. I sang "If My Friends Could See Me Now!" from *Sweet Charity* and thought I was going to faint with every word. All I could see through the whole audition was Phil smiling up at me from the second row. When I got back to my seat Jeff looked at me and grinned.

"You weren't half bad," he said.

"Thanks," I answered, as sarcastically as possible.

"No, I mean it. You used to sound all croaky . . . somewhat like a frog . . . now it's more like a cute crow."

"Oh, great."

Then Stimpson called Jeff's name and before he even began I started thinking up comparisons: an unoiled screen door . . . an untuned violin . . . a very old . . . but my imagination screeched to a halt. Phil Chrystie was sitting next to me again. I could feel him looking at me but I refused to look back. When Jeff finished, Phil tapped me on the shoulder.

"I'm sorry I called you Brenda before," he said. "I don't know where that came from. There's a Brenda in my English lit class but I hardly know her."

"That's okay. People are always doing that to me." I have no idea why I said that because people *never* did that to me. I guess it was because he looked so sincerely embarrassed. Just then Jeff came back to his seat.

"Do you two know each other?" I asked, knowing that, of course, they did.

"Yeah, sure," Jeff said.

"You're Jeff Grathwohl," Phil said, extending his hand.

For a moment I thought Jeff wasn't going to take his hand but then he did. It was a very brief handshake and Jeff pulled away as though Phil was Frankenstein's monster himself.

After all three of us just sat there for a few seconds, I turned to Jeff and said: "Your singing was very interesting. A bit like a billy goat dying of food poisoning." Before Jeff could get out the laugh that I could see he was trying to hold back, Phil leaned forward and across me.

"Oh no, Jeff . . . I thought it was quite nice, really." And then to me, "You shouldn't put people down like that, Camilla."

I started to open my mouth to tell him that it was just a game Jeff and I played but, unexpectedly, Jeff cut me off.

"I'm glad you said that, Phil. I've tried to tell her that for years. It's one of her worst defects."

I swung around to look at Jeff. I couldn't believe I was hearing right. He had a perfectly straight face. Then I heard Phil.

"I learned in my psych class this year that people who have the need to put others down all the time are basically insecure."

"I'm afraid that sums up our Cammy here," Jeff said.

Well it was more than I could stand! My best boy friend and the boy I loved attacking me in cold blood. I stood up.

"Excuse me," I said and pushed past Phil, walking calmly but deliberately down the aisle and out the door. I kept walking until I found myself on Route 25 headed toward home.

Now I have felt humiliation before in my life. I mean, it was not altogether a new sensation for me but somehow, as small a thing as it was, I couldn't remember ever feeling quite *so* humiliated. I suppose it was the two people involved because compared with the time in first grade when I wet my pants right through my skirt while sitting in the first row and everyone knew it, this was nothing. And really nothing compared to the time in the third grade when I was a leaf in the Fall Pageant and my costume fell off, leaving me on stage in full view of the audience in just my underwear. And, of course, there had been other humiliations over the years . . . but I truly couldn't remember ever having felt worse.

As I rounded the turn on 25 I could hear the sounds coming from the Strawberry Festival. I crossed the street and found myself heading through the parking lot toward the big tent. I guess my psychology of the moment was that as long as I was being treated like a creep—and as long as I felt like a creep—I might as well behave like a creep . . . and those are the last thoughts I remember as I raised a forkful of strawberry shortcake to my mouth . . . the first of seven pieces I would eat.

The only thing I wanted to do when I got home was lie on my bed and listen to Seals & Crofts but no such luck. I had completely forgotten that my mother had weekend guests. Naturally, by the time I got home at four, they had arrived. When I came in through the front door I could hear them laughing on the porch. Since the stairs are right near the door I would have been able to escape without anyone knowing I was home except that Bob Bennett, at that very moment, came from the kitchen through the pantry carrying a drink.

"Weeelll," he said in his booming voice, "there you are." He set his drink down and opened up his huge arms. There was no way out. When Bob Bennett wanted to hug you, you had no choice. I let myself be hugged and tried to act somewhat enthusiastic. On this particular occasion I wanted to be out of his grasp quicker than usual. The strawberry shortcake was not sitting too well. He finally let go.

"We've been waiting for you, Camilla. You look terrific."

"Thanks," I said. "So do you." He did not. He looked like an idiot. In the past year he had let his hair grow long and he insisted on wearing an Indian band around his forehead. Now as you can imagine, I have nothing against long hair . . . not even on old people . . . but Bob had very thin, oily hair and it hung in stringy bunches around his head and never looked clean. And the Indian band looked as though it had been dragged through a grease pit and just sort of stuck to his head. On top of that he was wearing an Indian shirt from India, love beads, and bermuda shorts with knee socks and sandals. It was as though he couldn't make up his mind what generation he belonged to, but to anyone looking at him it was clear that he was just post-Second World War, trying desperately to be post-Vietnam.

"We're all out on the porch," he said, putting a beefy arm around my shoulder and guiding me through the living room. "Look who's here!"

Mattie, his wife, turned her big-boned, red-haired self in her wicker chair, gave a little pig-squeal of pleasure, and rose to greet me. Kissing and hugging Bob was bad enough, but at least he didn't smell. Mattie did. It was always the same. Frying onions. It so happens I love the smell of frying onions— but not on a person. So when she came toward me, her muscular arms outstretched, I carefully and unobtrusively as possible held my breath.

"How are you, sweetie? You look terrific . . . doesn't she look terrific . . . really terrific . . . have you been to the tryouts? . . . Laura said you were trying out for some show . . . how'd you do?"

All this while she clutched me to her mammoth bosom. I had to answer—to say something—and to do that I had to breathe. There it was. Frying onions. I mumbled something about my audition and gently extricated myself from her suffocating grip. I once brought up the frying onion thing to my mother and she tried to tell me I was imagining it, but one time I heard her discussing Mattie with a friend and colleague and she was saying that Mattie's personal habits . . . I love that—Mattie's personal habits—Mattie's stink is what she meant . . . were as they were because, consciously or unconsciously, she wanted to keep Bob away from her. Well, I don't know if it kept him away or not but it certainly produced the desired effect from me. I moved away, looked out at the water, and took a deep breath, saying what a beautiful June day it was.

"You want to walk down to the beach, Cam?" Bob asked. "The kids are down there with a friend of ours."

I looked closer and I could see the two Bennett brats and a man. The oldest Bennett brat was six. Melissa. She behaved as though she was retarded (she wasn't) and never said anything. She always hid behind Mattie's legs or Bob's and peeked out at you and people were always saying things like: "What's wrong, Melissa, cat got your tongue?" in singsongy voices and Melissa would close her eyes and stick the tongue out at you and everyone would laugh. Personally, it made me sick. The other Bennett brat was Sandra and she was four. She was just the opposite from Melissa and never shut up. Even when you were trying to have a mature conversation she never shut up. The Bennetts did not believe in disciplining their brats and, consequently, when the brats were around an intelligent conversation was impossible. So the last thing in the world I wanted to do was walk down to the beach to see those two little horrors. But Bob Bennett rarely waited for an answer and I found myself going out the porch door and walking down the path with him before I knew what happened.

Bob was a Gestalt analyst and everything he did was under the guise of freedom and spontaneity. The only trouble was he never seemed to consider anybody's freedom and spontaneity but his own. The truth is, I'd always thought he was the least free person I'd ever known. He worked so hard at it.

When we got down to the beach the two brats ran up to Bob, and Sandra jumped up into his arms and Melissa hid behind his legs.

"Say hello to Camilla, kids. You remember Camilla, don't you?"

"Hel-looooo," Sandra said.

Melissa just peered out from behind his legs.

The man on the beach walked toward us.

"Ray, this is Laura's older daughter, Camilla."

"How do you do," he said, and I almost fainted.

He looked exactly like Steve McQueen.

"This is Ray Fowler."

I took his hand and he smiled. A lot of things went through my mind at once. He was good-looking, just the right age for my mother, and so far there was no Mrs. Fowler in sight. How fabulous to have a Steve McQueen type for a father. Then I realized I was doing my usual thing. Jeff would have had my head if he could have read my mind. He was forever after me for jumping the gun, planning ahead. "Live in the moment," Jeff always said and I knew he was right but I couldn't help myself. Obviously, this guy was here for the weekend and if there was no Mrs. Fowler, then he was here for my mother.

"How do you do, Mr. Fowler," I said.

"Call me Ray."

A good sign. He wanted to be friendly with me. If they liked my mother they always wanted to make friends with me and Rachel.

"Have you been in the water?" I asked.

"No, it's a little too cold for me."

"I was in the water," the younger Bennett brat butted in.

She was in jeans and a T-shirt and it was perfectly obvious that she hadn't been in, and to make that point Melissa gave her a push which sent her flying into the sand. Naturally, she started crying and throwing sand which hit all of us, and Bob nodded and watched and said something about letting them work it out. Ray moved between the flying sand and me and suggested we go up to the house while they worked it out.

As we walked up the path I asked him a series of questions. Was he an analyst too? No, he worked on Wall Street. Had he ever been to the North Fork before? No, it was his first time and he thought it was beautiful. Two pluses for him. How did he know the

Bennetts? Bob was once his analyst. A minus. And . . .
would Mrs. Fowler be joining him? There was no Mrs.
Fowler—at the moment. A super double plus. Divorced or widowed? Divorced. Good. Somehow divorced men were always more eager to marry again.
I guess widowers felt disloyal or something. Maybe
that had been Mother's trouble.

When we got to the porch Mother was putting out
some cheese and crackers and had a pitcher of martinis all ready. She poured one for Ray and I thought
when he took it from her that their eyes met and held
an instant longer than necessary. Then Rachel came
in and had to go through the routine with Mattie.
She'd get the Bob Bennett number later. I introduced
her to Ray as though he and I had been friends forever.

"Where'd you go in the middle of tryouts, Cam?
Miss Stimpson wanted to hear you again."

"She did?"

"Yeah. She called your name a couple of times
and nobody knew where you went."

"Well, I'll go back tomorrow."

"She said she wanted everyone back. Where'd ya
go?"

"I had some errands I had to run," I said.

"What errands?"

"Personal things," I said, and glanced over at Ray
who was staring at my mother. She really was nice-
looking for an older woman. Even though she'd
turned forty on her last birthday there were times
when you could almost say she was glamorous. Jeff
thought she looked like Elizabeth Montgomery but
I couldn't see it. Anyway, Ray was staring at her but,
she, poor devil, was having her ear bent by Mattie
so she didn't notice Ray's passionate look. I figured
that now I had gone through all the social things, I
could easily disappear for an hour or so before dinner. My Seals & Crofts mood was gone and I was
into a Gilbert O'Sullivan phase. I could almost hear
him in my mind. "Alone Again (Naturally)" was the

only thing I could bear to hear at that moment. I excused myself and as I was heading for my room I heard my mother yell after me.

"Camilla, don't eat anything. Bob and Mattie stopped at the festival and we have tons of strawberry shortcake for dessert . . . so don't spoil your appetite."

It was all I could do to make it upstairs to the bathroom.

Chapter 6

~~~~~~~~~~~~~~~~~~~~~~~~~~~~

Dinner was a disaster! Bob Bennett, as usual, domi-
nated the conversation, raving on and on about open
marriages and how free he and Mattie were and how
they both slept with other people and nobody was
jealous or anything. And Mattie, who was stinking
more than ever, sat next to me, making my already ten-
der stomach churn with every breath, twinkling and
punctuating what Bob said with little grunts. Ray,
I think, was slightly embarrassed by the conversation
because he kept his eyes on his plate, and Mother
drank an extra amount of wine and seemed kind of
silly to me. Melissa spent most of the dinner hour under the table, her eyes occasionally appearing at the
table ledge, and Sandra just chatted on about God
knows what. Rachel and I said very little. Frankly, I
thought the whole thing was kind of repulsive—not because I'm a prude or anything, but because I thought
it was all a fantastic lie. I mean, who in their right
mind would sleep with either one of those two? As
far as I was concerned they were extraordinarily
lucky to have each other.

Fortunately, just as I took my last difficult mouthful of food the phone rang and it was for me.

"Is this the cute crow?" It was Jeff, of course.

I was silent for a few seconds as the memory of my
humiliation surged up in me again. "What do *you*
want?"

"That's a nice thing to say to your best friend."

45

"You have a funny idea about friendship," I said.

"Oh, come on, Camel . . . where's your sense of humor?"

"In Chicago for the weekend." That was a thing Jeff and I had between us. Quite a while ago we noticed that adults were always asking that kind of question about inanimate objects, like "How's your new house?" or "How's your new car?" It always made us laugh and want to respond with something like: "Oh, it's got a bad cold this week" or referring to the house: "Not so good, it's getting a divorce."

"Got me," Jeff said. "Hey, Cam, you're not really mad at me, are you?"

"Yes, I think I really am."

"I was just fooling around."

"Well, it was very embarrassing."

"In front of that goop?" he said, clearly astonished. Sometimes Jeff was amazingly insensitive.

"If you don't understand then I can't explain it to you."

There was silence and then he said: "Do you really dig him?"

I had always told Jeff everything but something made me hesitate this time. "It's just that I don't know him and I didn't like being treated that way in front of a stranger. . . . I mean, he doesn't know the way we are with each other."

"Okay, okay. I'm sorry. I guess I'm guilty of getting a laugh at your expense." That was something Jeff and I never did. We both had what could be called a keen sense of humor but we agreed that getting a laugh at someone else's expense was definitely not funny. The so-called wits in school were always doing that kind of thing. You know, taking the creepiest kid in school and putting him in some embarrassing situation or something. It was the kind of thing Bruce McDonald was always doing. Like last year when he took Paul Freeman's briefcase (nobody but creeps carry briefcases) and threw it out the window and everybody went wild with laughter when Paul broke down and cried. Everybody except Jeff, who went downstairs and got the briefcase and gave it back to Paul. A lot of kids thought Jeff was a creep to do that and, of course, they voted Bruce wittiest of his homeroom. Jeff believed that if you were truly witty you didn't have to hurt anyone to get a laugh, so I knew that he was really sorry about what he'd done today.

"I'm sure you didn't mean to do it," I said.

"I really didn't, Cam. I *am* sorry. FF?"

That was forgive and forget. "Sure."

"Everybody's going to the drive-in. *The Other* is playing with some other horror flick. Want to go?"

"I've seen *The Other*. It's cruddy. Are you going?"

"Yeah, I think so. Affectionate Al is having his poker game tonight so I might as well make myself scarce."

As I indicated before, Jeff called his father that for his lack of affection. He couldn't remember his father every touching him. On the other hand, Jeff's mother is too affectionate, as far as I'm concerned. She was always making a big fuss over him and kissing him and, frankly, it embarrassed me. But Jeff was devoted to his mother so I never said anything about it.

"I think I'll just stay home," I said. My stomach was feeling really lousy and I thought I'd better go to bed early so I'd feel okay for the next set of tryouts.

"You sure?"

"I'm sure."

"Okay, well . . . I'll pick you up at twelve thirty tomorrow, okay?"

"Sure."

A short silence. "Hey, you know what?"

"What?"

"You know what the longest song title ever was? It was 'I'm a Cranky Old Yank in a Clanky Old Tank on the Streets of Yokohama with My Honolulu Mama Doin' Those Beat-o, Beat-o, Flat-on-My-Seat-O, Hirohito Blues.' "

"You made that up."

"Nope. Hoagy Carmichael, 1943. See you tomorrow."

After I hung up, I went back to the dining room and said I hoped that no one would mind but I was going to excuse myself because I wanted a good night's sleep for the next day. Naturally, Bob had an objection.

"Oh, no, Cam. I've got a whole raft of new games to play."

Bob loved to play games. Not board games or good games like Bartlett's or Dictionary or Botticelli but psychological games. Encounter-type games. I think he liked to try them out on his friends before he used them in his group therapy sessions. Whatever it was, I hated them because, no matter what, they always ended up with people telling the truth about each other in the cruelist possible way and someone always started crying. Actually, it was usually Bob who told the truth and Mattie who ended up crying.

"Gee," I said, "ordinarily I'd love to, but it's very important that I get my rest tonight."

"Oh, come on, it's only eight o'clock. Just one or two games. I've got this dandy new one where two people . . ."

Fortunately my mother came to my rescue. "I think if Camilla feels she should get some sleep, she knows best, Bob."

"I guess so," he said sulkily and he slid down in his chair, looking exactly like Melissa, who was slumped next to him.

Upstairs I got into bed with my earphones and listened to Carole King. I closed my eyes and thought about Phil as Carole sang "You Light Up My Life."

You light up my life like sunrise in the morning
You make me believe anything is possible
I didn't have a dream to my name
Darkness was mine, it was such a shame

But you came to light up my life
You brought me faith, and hope, and love, and light.

By the time she got to the line "Loving you's left
me with nothing to conceal," the tears were streaming
down my face. This may be hard to understand . . . I
mean, why I was reacting like that. Because the
truth of the matter was that I *always* believed anything was possible and I had *lots* of dreams and I had
plenty to conceal. But the thing of it was that I
could imagine how I *would* feel if I loved Phil the
way I did and I *had* felt all those things. I have a fabulous imagination and by the time the song was over
I was sobbing into my pillow so loud that I could
barely hear the words to the next song. It was one
of the best Saturday nights I had had in a long
time.

A lot more kids showed up for Sunday's auditions,
and among them was Maura Harris. Penny sat down
beside me and pulled her crew cap down over her
eyes.

"My life is over," she said.

"What's up?"

"It's not what's up, it's whats' *here*. M.H. to be
exact."

"You knew she was trying out, Pen."

"There's knowing and there's knowing, if you know
what I mean. Tell me the truth, Cam," she said, turning the brim of the hat up so her big round eyes
peeked out from below. "Do you think she's better-
looking than I am? I can take it if you do. Don't be
afraid to speak the truth."

"Well . . ."

"Never mind."

"I was going to say that you're very different types."

"Ugly and pretty." She pulled down the brim.

"Come on, Penny, you know you're not ugly. You're
very cute."

"And Maura?"

"Well, I don't think she's pretty."

"Now let's talk about talent."

"I think you're terrific."

"And Maura?"

"I don't get her message."

Just then Stimpson called Maura's name and she went up on stage. Maura could sight-read so she sang one of the songs from the show, "Blow, Gabriel, Blow." Well, to tell the truth, I was prepared to hate her, particularly with Penny sitting next to me and groaning all through the song, but I couldn't. It wasn't that she had such a spectacular voice . . . I mean it was nothing like Tina's. But there was something . . . something you couldn't put your finger on. Like not being able to take your eyes off her while she sang. There was something about the way she moved and smiled. She had self-confidence, I guess. At any rate, it was a lot different from Penny, who had kept grabbing at her throat and rolling her eyes in different directions when she'd come to the high notes.

You could have heard a flea sneeze during Maura's tryout. When it was over nobody clapped but everybody broke into an instant buzz of conversation. I glanced over at Jeff who was sitting by himself and he had the most unbelievable smile on his face . . . like he was proud of her or something. I was going to have to find out if he was digging her.

"Well?" Penny croaked.

"Well, what?"

"What do you think?"

"You have a better voice." And she did . . . technically.

"But?"

"No buts."

"You think I have a chance?" she asked, straightening up.

"Of course you do."

"Oh, Cam," she said, "I know I'm always foolin' around and everything, but seriously, I've never wanted anything so much in my life. Last night I even prayed. I haven't done that since I was six months old."

"You'll get it," I said and tried desperately to sound convincing because I really wasn't sure anymore.

When all the singing auditions were over (Stimpson asked me to try one of Bonnie's songs, but I can't sight-read so she said it was okay and not to worry), we started the readings. I had absolutely no trouble with the part of Bonnie. It was as though it was made for me. Stimpson had Penny, Tina, and Maura read for the part of Reno and once again there was something about Maura that was riveting. It wasn't that Penny wasn't good. She was. But it didn't get you the way Maura's reading did. Then Maura and Penny both read for Bonnie and I started to get a sinking feeling. Either one of them could have played the part with ease. Especially Maura. So if Penny did get the part of Reno probably Maura would get Bonnie and then I'd be back in the chorus like last year. Or if it was the other way around! Surely Stimpson wasn't going to stick Penny in the chorus! Why hadn't it occurred to me before? The third female lead, the part of Hope, would undoubtedly go to Tina. I mean she was the typical ingenue type and the only one who could sing "All Through the Night" and "It's Delovely." So that would leave me in the chorus or swinging a paintbrush. To quote Penny: My life was over.

When we left the theater, knowing that Stimpson would be calling us later that evening if we got a part, not even the fact that Phil walked me to Jeff's car could console me.

"I thought you were excellent in the readings, Camilla."

"Thank you."

"I'm sure Miss Stimpson thought so, too."

"I hope so."

"Well, I'd better get back inside to help out with the casting. I'll see you both on Monday."

"Year, sure," Jeff said.

I could barely get out a good-bye as I shut the car door.

"Where do you want to wait it out . . . your house or mine?"

"Is there anybody home at your house?" He shook his head. "Then let's go there. My house is jumping with jerks." He started the car and slowly we drove off to endure the longest three hours of my life.

Chapter 7

As soon as the phone rang at Jeff's house, telling him that he had the non-singing role of Mr. Whitney, I hugged him and ran through the yards to my house. Fortunately, the guests had left and Mother was taking a nap and Rachel wasn't around. I paced back and forth in the hallway, staring at the wall phone, willing it to ring and, finally, it did. I let it ring twice so I wouldn't seem too anxious.

"Camilla, this is Susan Stimpson."

"Hi, Miss Stimpson," I said, as coolly as possible.

"I'd like you to play the part of Bonnie."

The most beautiful words I'd ever heard. I wanted to scream, to throw the phone in the air, to kiss Stimpson right through the phone, but I didn't do any of those things. A person has to be cool in a situation like that.

"Oh, fine," I said, with as little emotion in my voice as possible.

"Is something wrong, Camilla?" she asked.

"Wrong? No, of course not."

"You *do* want to play the part, don't you?"

Maybe I'd gone too far in my coolness. "Oh yes, I'm . . . I'm very happy."

"Good. Well, I'll see you tomorrow at seven thirty."

"Miss Stimpson?"

"Call me Susan."

"Yes, Susan . . . I wondered, would it be out of order for me to ask who got the part of Reno?"

53

"No, it's not out of order, but I haven't reached her yet so I'd rather she knew first."

"Oh, yeah, sure. Okay, thank you."

When I hung up I sat there for a few moments and then I couldn't help myself . . . I just let out a huge yelp. In a second or two Mother was at the top of the stairs.

"Camilla?"

I ran to the bottom of the stairs. "I got the part, Mom."

"You scared me. Honey, that's just marvelous. I'm very proud of you."

And she was. I'm extremely lucky to have a mother who really cares about what I do and my happiness and all that stuff. But, sometimes, like all mothers, she just doesn't have any soul. I mean, can you believe that she actually expected me to eat dinner? We hassled about that a few minutes, until I convinced her that I was meeting with all the kids later and we'd have hamburgers. Actually, it was partially true. We were all meeting at Fisherman's at eight thirty but we'd probably be having pizza. I didn't want to tell her that because mothers don't think of pizza as real food.

I quickly ran back to Jeff's. Affectionate Al and the Dragon Lady were home by now. They were all sitting at the table and the D.L. was pushing Jeff's hair out of his eyes. At least that's what she wanted it to look like—the truth was that she was stroking his hair.

"Isn't it wonderful that Jeffrey got a speaking part this year?" she said to me when I walked in.

"It's terrific," I said. Naturally, she didn't ask about me. She hated me, I think, because Jeff spent so much time with me.

Jeff opened his mouth to ask me if I'd heard but Affectionate Al cut him off.

"It's a lot of crap, if you ask me," he grumbled.

"Oh, Albert," the D.L. said.

"A bunch of queers," he mumbled and left the room.

Jeff started bitting his lip, which he almost always did when he was around his father.

"Pay no attention to him, darling . . . he doesn't understand these things."

"So?" Jeff finally said to me.

"I got it."

He jumped up and out of the grasp of the D.L., ran around the table, and hugged me. "Super," he said.

"Congratulations," the D.L. said.

"Thank you, Mrs. Grathwohl."

"Is it a good part?"

"Speaking and singing," I said.

"Oh, how nice," she said coldly.

After a few more icy exchanges with the D.L. we got out of there.

"Have you heard from Penny?" I asked as we walked to Jeff's Volkswagen.

"I called her but her brother answered and said she was occupied. *Occupied*, for God's sake. What do you suppose that means?"

"Maybe she was in the bathroom."

"Slitting her wrists?"

I shrugged and told him about my exchange with Stimpson about the Reno Sweeney part. We got in the car.

"Camilla," he said, "I'm sure she didn't get it . . . Maura was much better. You saw that, didn't you?"

I didn't know what to say. I didn't want to be disloyal to Penny and I didn't want to lie to Jeff either. "Maybe you're prejudiced," I said.

"What's that supposed to mean?"

"Nothing."

"Oh, don't give me that."

"Well, it just seems that, lately, you've been awfully pro-Maura."

"And?"

"And, well . . . tell me the truth, Jeff—do you want to make it with her?"

With that he started to laugh like I hadn't seen him laugh in years. Finally, he pulled himself together and started the car.

"Is that supposed to be an answer?"

"I don't even know her," he said. "I just think she's very talented, that's all."

"So why is it so funny?"

"You wouldn't understand."

It was as though he'd slapped me across the face. In all the hundred years we'd been friends, Jeff had never said that to me about anything. In fact, it was usually the opposite. I can't tell you how many times he said I was the only person who understood him. All the happiness in getting the part of Bonnie just went right out of me like I was balloon he'd pricked. We rode the eight minutes to Fisherman's in silence.

Janet, Mary El, Walt, and Tina were at the table when we got there. By their expressions, I could tell that there was bad news.

"She didn't get it, did she?" I asked.

"You guessed it," Janet said.

Jeff and I sat down.

"How is she?"

"Going through some changes, I guess. Sam is with her. Congratulations to you both, though."

Then we all exchanged congratulations. Tina had gotten the part of Hope, Mary El had gotten the part of Mrs. Harcourt, Hope's mother, and Walt had gotten the part of Moonface Martin, which was the only surprise. Sam had gotten Sir Evelyn . . . we all knew he would because he was the only boy who could do an English accent . . . and this new boy, Eben Clay, whom none of us knew, had gotten the male lead, Billy Crocker.

"How is Bruce taking that?" I asked.

"He's probably out getting drunk somewhere," Walt said.

We had all thought Bruce McDonald would get the part of Billy because he was an all-American type and had this really super voice.

"How come Bruce didn't get it?" I asked Janet.

"Well, his reading was pretty bad, you know, and

he's a baritone and Billy's a tenor. I think Eben will be best for the part," Janet said, smiling a kind of secret smile. Knowing Jan as well as I did, I knew that before long she'd be getting a crush on Eben. He *was* good-looking. Tall and dark with very blue eyes and white teeth.

"Did Stimpson put Penny in the chorus?" Jeff asked.

"No, she gave her the part of one of the Angels. Chastity, I think. No one knows if she'll accept or not. She told Stimpson she'd think about it. The Angels are pretty good parts. There're four of them."

At that point our pizzas came and everything got silent as we dug in. As I was about to bite into my second piece, I looked up at Walt and stopped, my pizza hanging in midair.

"Je-sus!" said Walt, who was facing the door.

We all turned. Coming slowly into the dining room was a figure all in black. She was wearing a long black denim skirt, a black turtleneck, and a black cowboy hat. It was Penny. She was leaning on Sam's arm as she approached us. Janet and Mary El got two more chairs and pulled them up to the table. Sam helped Penny into her chair and sat down next to her. None of us could think of anything to say. Finally, Penny took out a cigarette, stuck it into a long black holder, and spoke in a very low kind of whisper.

"It is a far, far better thing I do than I have ever done before."

We all glanced at each other and waited for her to go on. But she didn't.

Then Walt said, "What is it you're going to do?"

"I have only one life to give for Youth On Stage and I will give it as . . . an Angel." She cleared her throat. "As God is my witness, I will back and support Maura Harris in the difficult role of Reno Sweeney."

"This we know," Janet said.

"You want some pizza?" Mary El asked.

"No . . . no thank you . . . food is not for me on this night . . . truly the darkest night of my career."

"What career?" Walt asked and Tina poked him in the ribs with her elbow.

"How about a Coke?" Sam asked.

"The only thing I could drink on this occasion would be absinthe."

Mary El started calling for the waitress until someone told her what absinthe was.

"I'm really sorry, Pen," I said.

"Thank you," she said, softly and a bit coldly, I thought. It occurred to me then that she was probably a little miffed at me because I'd gotten the part of Bonnie and I felt slightly guilty.

"Have you eaten anything at all today?" Janet asked.

"Dear friend," she said, "try and understand. Food is the last thing in this world that I can think of right now."

We all nodded and nobody ate. Except Walt.

"Well, food is something I can always think of." He picked up a slice and started munching. I was really hungry but I watched the pizza turn cold on my plate because I felt too guilty to eat. I guess the others did too. I mean, the truth of the matter was, Penny had gotten the smallest part of any of us and under those circumstances I thought she was taking it very well. Suddenly, she rose.

"I must leave you now. . . . I know how joyous you all must be having gotten such nice parts." She glanced at me on that one. "And I know that having me around on this occasion is a lousy downer."

Well, of course, we tried to convince her that wasn't true, even though it was, and begged her to stay but she was adamant.

"No, no, dear friends . . . I must be alone tonight. Celebrate . . . be merry . . . I will see you on the morrow."

She swept out, Sam rolling his eyes as he followed her through the dining room. When she was gone, as if on signal, everyone dove into the pizza, cold as it was.

After we left Fisherman's we drove around in Walt's car for a while trying to sing and celebrate, but Penny had dampened all our spirits and no matter how we tried we just couldn't get it together.

About ten we separated and went home. Jeff and I didn't sit in the car and rap as usual—I didn't feel much like talking to him after what he'd said earlier and I guess he was feeling worse about Penny than anyone. After all, he'd practically predicted it.

I listened to the Moody Blues for a while, feeling just awful about Penny and imagining her lying in her room . . . alone . . . depressed . . . hungry. By the time the phone rang I was practically in a state of deep despair.

"Camilla . . . it's Sam."

"How is she?" I said quickly.

"Oh, she's okay. Wait till I tell—"

"Sam," I said, "we have to give her a lot of love and attention . . . and we've got to make sure she eats."

"Are you kidding?" he said. "When we left you guys she insisted I drive her to Riverhead to McDonald's, where she promptly devoured two Big Macs, an order of fries, and a chocolate drink. And she took an order of French fried onions home with her."

"Oh, thank God," I said.

Right before I fell asleep I had a tiny flash of anger as I thought of Penny's menu that night and remembered the cold, clammy taste of my pizza. Oh, well, that's show biz!

Chapter 8

~~~~~~~~~~~~~~~~~~~~~~~~~~~~~~~~~

Monday the 25th of June was the beginning of a lot of
things for me. Not only was I going to start rehearsals
but it was the start of my summer job. It was not
something I was looking forward to. I was going to be
a checker in the A&P. I had already gone in one
afternoon the week before for some training—or,
rather, orientation, as Mr. Griggs, the manager, liked
to call it. Have you ever noticed how people with
basically dumb jobs take them so seriously? I suppose
if they didn't they'd have to admit how dumb they
were and then they'd have to kill themselves or something. Anyway, Mr. Griggs was one of these people.
He was a huge man with a crew cut which made him
look pinheaded and he had a very high, squeaky
voice. It was hard not to burst into hysterics when he
talked to you because the voice was so out of place
with the body. And, to top it all off, he was very, very
formal.

"All right, Miss Crawford, I think we are prepared
now to begin the orientation. First we will peruse
the stock so you may familiarize yourself with the
products. Attention! Follow me, please."

All that in a voice that was higher than mine. He'd
taken me up and down all the aisles to memorize
where everything was.

"Pay careful attention to where each item is located,
Miss Crawford. There will be questions later."

And there were.

"Spices, Miss Crawford—quickly."

"Ahhh . . . aisle 3."

"Tomato juice, please. Quickly, quickly. The customer does not want to wait around all day for your memory to focus."

On and on. Then I had to learn the cash register. If you've ever used a cash register then you know how simple it is. But you would have thought he was teaching me how to use the most complicated computer ever invented. And, as for making change, that was no problem either because the register does it automatically. But Griggs was one of those people who had to make everything more difficult than it actually was. Basically, that's all there was to the job except that, occasionally, I'd be asked to mark stock and put things on shelves. At the end of the "orientation," Griggs shook my hand and pinned me. I couldn't believe it!

"You will, Miss Crawford, wear this button at all times when on duty."

I looked down at the button he'd just pinned on me. It was green with white lettering and said: *Weeeeeo!*

"I hope you will be happy as a member of our A&P WEO family. We are happy to have you aboard. See you promptly at eight forty-five on the twenty-fifth. Good day."

So you can understand why I wasn't too anxious to start my career as a WEO checker! (In case you don't know, WEO stands for "Where Economy Originates" and is the latest A&P advertising campaign.) The only thing that was going to make it bearable was that Sam worked there too. The thing that would make it really unbearable was that Maura Harris was a member of the A&P WEO family. I certainly wasn't looking forward to seeing her that first morning.

Griggs was waiting at the door for us.

"Good morning, Miss Crawford, Mr. Ahlers. Are we all ready to begin our A&P WEO life?"

Can you imagine anything more depressing than an A&P WEO life? Griggs put me on Register Two and took Sam back to the Dairy Department.

At nine o'clock on the button the beasts entered. "Beasts" was how I was to come to think of the shoppers. I had never realized how impatient, how rude, how hideously awful people could be. I also never realized how *boring* a job could be. After only an hour it was clear to me that my A&P WEO life was indeed going to be soul-destroying.

Maura was on a later shift so I didn't see her until after lunch.

"Hi, guy," she said. "How do you like the A&P WEO life?"

"Thrilling."

"The only way to survive is to make your mind a complete blank. Otherwise, you'll end up on the funny farm."

"Thanks for the tip."

She gave me a funny little salute and started to walk away.

"Maura? Congratulations."

"Oh, thanks," she said, and kept going.

Can you imagine? Oh, thanks! Not a word about me. Maura was exactly what I thought she was. An egomaniac!

I told Sam about it while we waited for his mother to pick us up.

"Well, maybe she didn't know you got the part," he said.

"She could have asked."

"And suppose you *hadn't* gotten a part? That would be pretty embarrassing wouldn't it?"

"I suppose," I said. "But there are ways of asking. She could have said: How did the other kids do? Or something like that. The reason she didn't is because she didn't care. She only cares about herself. She's a raving egomaniac."

"You don't know what an egomaniac is until you've spent an hour with my father."

"I *have* spent an hour with your father. More than an hour."

"Do you know what he did last night? When I got home . . ."

"But don't you think Maura . . ."

"Camilla," he said, "I'm telling you about my father."

"Okay . . . shoot." As Sam started in on the insanity of his father, I realized he was the worst person in the world to discuss egomania with.

Rehearsal began at seven thirty. Stimpson wore a whistle around her neck and when she blew it we all stopped what we were doing immediately. She told us all to sit down. Then she made a little speech about the pot and booze thing saying that if anyone, even a lead, did either of those things, even if it was the night before opening, he or she would be thrown out. I thought I saw her give Maura a special look, but I couldn't be sure. She said she meant it and not to bother testing her. I, for one, believed her. Next, she told everyone with a speaking part to go to the back of the theater and form a circle and those people who were going to be in the chorus to sit up front with Jane Hammand, who was our musical director.

When we formed our circle, Phil Chrystie put his chair next to mine. In one way I couldn't have been happier but, in another, I wished he hadn't. I was afraid that sitting close to him during the reading of the play would make me nervous and I'd sound awful. As it turned out, his proximity made me try all the harder to be good.

We read the first act, which seemed pretty funny, and then we took a five-minute break.

"Do you like the play?" Phil asked me.

"It's hard to tell, but I think so. It's pretty crazy."

"I think it's going to be fun to do . . . and you're going to be really good as Bonnie."

"Really?"

"Sure. I can tell from the reading that when you get into it you'll be really funny."

"Thanks, Phil."

He looked at me a moment and smiled. Then he said: "What are you doing after rehearsal?"

We'd all planned to go to Fisherman's, but it sounded like maybe he was going to ask me to do something with him so I just kind of shrugged my shoulders.

"Janet asked me to join the kids at Fisherman's— aren't you going?"

Damn Janet! You'd think she'd have the decency to let me in on these things. "Oh, that's right," I said, trying to cover. "I forgot about that."

He nodded just as Stimpson blew her whistle and everybody got ready to start the second act.

When we finished, Stimpson said it had been a good first reading. I'd like to tell you what *Anything Goes* is about but it's a little too complicated to explain. It takes place on an ocean liner going to England in the 1930's and all these crazy characters are aboard, getting mixed up with each other. I played the moll of a gangster who doesn't make the ship, and so I end up with Moonface Martin, another gangster who's disguised as a missionary. Then there's this Englishman who . . . It's no use, you'll just have to take my word for it. It's pretty funny and the music is great. Sam was going to do the makeup and he said he'd get me this really neat trashy-looking platinum wig and I could wear lots of eye stuff and rouge. And my costumes were going to be tight-fitting and flashy and really wonderfully disgusting. I could hardly wait.

When we got to Fisherman's, Jeff sat on one side of me and Phil on the other. There had been an empty chair next to Janet but he chose to sit next to me. I hoped Janet wouldn't notice but she rarely missed anything.

We were all discussing the play and how funny it could be and then Phil said:

"You're all going to be terrific, but you're damn

lucky to have Maura; she's going to make it really work."

Naturally, there was a dead silence as everybody tried not to look at Penny.

He went on: "By the way, where is she?"

"What do you mean, where is she?" Janet asked.

"Well, I mean, how come she's not here?"

"Uhhh, she didn't come," Sam said.

Phil smiled. "I can see that. Why not?"

"Because," Jeff said out of the corner of his mouth, "she wasn't asked to come." He lit one cigarette from another.

"Oh. Don't you like Maura?"

"This is really gross," Mary El mumbled.

"She's not one of our all-time favorites," Walt said.

"You mean," Phil said, "that you're purposely excluding her? Frankly, I think that's pretty lousy—she is one of . . ."

"Do you know who made the first single gold record?" Jeff asked.

"No, who?" Walt was as eager to change the subject as everyone else.

"Alma Gluck. She recorded 'Carry Me Back to Old Virginny' on the Red Seal label."

We all pretended we were very interested in this information and started asking Jeff lots of questions about it. Then Phil interrupted.

"Excuse me, Jeff," he said. "It's true that Alma Gluck sold over a million copies of that single, but it wasn't literally a golden record. The first official golden record was Glenn Miller's 'Chattanooga Choo Choo.' "

Well, you can imagine the reaction to that. First there was silence and then Walt started laughing and then Jeff's face turned red. I really felt sorry for him. I mean, often people questioned his facts but nobody had ever been in a position to correct him before.

"Are you sure?" Jeff asked.

"Yes. I can show it to you in the *Guinness Book of World Records.*"

"I can look it up myself," Jeff said.

"Oh, Jeff-baby," Walt said, "it looks like you've met your match."

"I doubt that," Jeff said in a very snotty way.

Penny changed the subject by asking when we'd have our first party. We all got very interested in that—except of course, for Jeff, who just slid way down in his chair and stared at his Coke.

When it was time for us to go, Phil turned to me.

"Can I give you a ride home, Camilla?"

Before I could get the *yes* out of my mouth, Jeff interrupted.

"That's okay," he said. "We live right next door to each other."

"Oh . . . oh, sure," Phil said.

I could have killed Jeff right there on the spot.

On the way home I kept counting to ten, trying not to scream or punch him or something, and then I remembered that my mother was always saying that it's good to let your anger out so I just yelled: "WHY?"

I guess I scared him because he swerved the car. "Jesus, Cam, what's wrong with you?"

"What's wrong with *me*? What's wrong with *you* is more like it."

"Nothing's wrong with me."

"Are you kidding? Why did you do that?"

"I don't know what you're talking about."

Now *that* was the most hateful thing about Jeff. Whenever he didn't want to talk about something he'd pull that one. Suddenly, he'd have no memory or act as though he'd had a lobotomy in the last ten minutes or something. And it was no use saying Yes, you do, Jeff, you know exactly what I'm talking about, because he'd just go on playing dumb until you pinned him down. So, instead of playing his game, I got right to the point.

"Why did you say to Phil that we live right next door to each other?"

"Well, don't we?"

Did you ever want to murder anyone with your bare hands? "Jeff, he was going to give me a ride home and you spoiled it and you know it."

"You mean, you wanted that jerk to give you a ride home? I thought I was doing you a favor."

"No, you didn't. You know very well that I . . . I . . ."

"You what?"

"I like him."

He started laughing. "Oh, come on, Camel, you couldn't possibly mean that."

"Well, I *do* mean it and you *know* it. You purposely ruined my chances with him. On top of everything else he's going to think I'm your girl."

"I doubt it," he said, in that snotty way again.

"Thanks. Look, Jeff, I don't know what's been bugging you these past few days but if you don't want to talk about it, I can't help you."

"Help me?"

"Something is making you really hateful."

We pulled into my driveway.

"I'm sorry if I haven't been living up to your high standards."

"Oh, come on, stop acting like I'm making things up. You know you've been acting peculiar."

"What do you mean peculiar?"

That was another thing he did to stall for time. He'd pick up on a word and make you define it.

"Okay, Jeff . . . once again, you don't want to talk. I'm not going to spend the whole night out here pulling teeth with you. If you want to talk I'll be glad to listen forever but . . ."

"There's nothing to talk about," he said, lighting his thousandth cigarette of the night.

"Okay, if that's the way you want it." I opened my door. "But I'll tell you this, if you interfere with me and Phil again, our friendship is over."

"And I'll tell *you* this," he said, getting angry, "if you're going to start hanging around with that *creep*, our friendship is over."

"Are you serious?"

"Perfectly."

"Since when do you care who I date?"

"I've always cared. You think I like to see my best friend going out with creeps?"

"You never cared about Harlan and he's a creep."

"You were younger then."

"What's that got to do with it?"

"Everything."

I knew I wasn't going to get anything more out of him and we just glared at one another. I got out of the car. "I have to live my own life," I said and slammed the door. Jeff took off like a maniac.

He was definitely going through changes. I couldn't get him to talk but I couldn't just abandon him either. If he hadn't said Phil was a creep days ago I would have thought he was just reacting to Phil correcting his golden disc facts. Jeff and I rarely fought and, when we did, it always made me feel sick. My mother had brought me up to discuss things freely . . . to keep the channels of communication open, so having Jeff as a friend was sometimes a strain. But I had learned that although it was hard for him to talk, almost impossible sometimes, eventually, even if it was weeks later, he would talk about what was bothering him. But something about this seemed different and I couldn't put my finger on it. I mean, why should he care if I wanted to date Phil? Even if he thought Phil was the most horrible person in the world surely Jeff knew I wasn't about to give up my career and run off and get married or anything. So what possible difference could it make? Could Jeff's feelings about me be changing? Impossible. We knew each other much too well. Maybe it was because he thought if I got involved with Phil I wouldn't be spending any time with him and since he wasn't dating anyone he'd be lonely. But then, what about Maura? No matter what he said, I still thought he dug Maura. But what did he mean when he said that I wouldn't understand?

I realized while I brushed my teeth that I wasn't any closer to the answers but I did have one very strong feeling. I don't know exactly why, but I felt that the summer stretching before me was not going to be the fun-and-games summer I had in mind. Something strange was going to happen.

Chapter 9

By Friday night, the last rehearsal of the first week, I was beginning to think all my suspicions and apprehensions had been for nothing. Rehearsals were going smoothly and Stimpson had only lost her temper once. Phil Chrystie had started hanging around with our crowd and even though he kept paying attention to me, Jeff didn't seem to notice. At least he acted as though the argument we'd had on Monday had never happened. Penny was feeling much better about things because Stimpson asked her to be Maura's understudy. Maura was still being Maura and Phil kept urging us to include her in our after-rehearsal gatherings but so far we hadn't. As much as I didn't like Maura, the fact that Phil was being so kind made me love him even more. He said the reason Maura was so standoffish was because she was shy. Janet, who would do anything Phil wanted, was planning to ask Maura to join us tonight. Sometimes I thought Janet was more in love with him than I was but I knew that he only liked her as a friend and even though he hadn't asked me out, I knew he wanted to and, eventually, he would. I guess he understood Maura's shyness . . . if she was . . . because he was basically shy too.

Sam had suffered a trauma in the middle of the week because Linda, the older woman he was in love with, stopped by his house and spent an hour talking with him. He was sure she was not in love with Burt, the man she was engaged to, and that he had been stupid not to take the opportunity to try and kiss her or something. Naturally, when Sam goes into these Linda depressions, Mary El goes into them too. Sam depressions, that is.

And Walt and Tina had broken up. It was all very amicable. They both admitted they were really wrong for each other' and that they were just staying together for convenience. Tina said Walt was a nice guy but she couldn't really love a clown. (Walt actually put lampshades on his head at parties sometimes.) And Walt said Tina was a nice girl but she'd lost her sense of humor somewhere and anyone who couldn't appreciate the Marx Brothers was from another planet. It looked as if Tina and Eben would be an item pretty soon and Walt didn't seem to mind.

So, even though a lot had happened in a short time, all my feelings of creepy things to come were not justified. At least not until that Friday night.

Jeff and I arrived right on the dot of seven thirty and a few of the chorus kids were still sitting on the steps.

"Hi, Sue," I said, "rehearsal hasn't started yet?"

"Maura's not here yet. Hi, Jeff . . . that's a cool shirt you're wearing."

"Thanks."

We went in.

"Sue Rice has a crush on you, Jeff."

"So?"

"Sew buttons," I said.

He gave me a look . . . like: You can do better than that. And I suppose I could but it got so boring waiting for Jeff to respond to someone. I was beginning to hope that he really *was* interested in Maura—she was better than no one.

When Stimpson saw us come in she said that we'd start with a scene we could do without Maura. While we blocked the scene I could tell something was going on in the theater but I didn't want to pay attention to it because Stimpson was very big on concentration, so in one way, I was surprised to see what I saw when the scene was over—and in another, I wasn't at all.

Most of the kids were sitting on the left-hand side of the orchestra, and Maura and a guy I'd never seen before . . . at least not off the local sports pages . . . were sitting on the right-hand side. A lot of the kids were staring at them and almost everybody was whispering.

Stimpson gave us a five-minute break and I came down the steps and sat next to Jeff.

"What's happening?" I asked him.

"Haven't you got eyes?"

"You mean Maura and . . . and . . . what's-his-name?"

"What's-his-name is Hank Allen—the big jock from Greenport."

You see, all the fuss was because Hank Allen is black. I suppose I should go into a rap here about blacks on the North Fork. First of all, there are hardly any—except for the ones in the Greenport ghetto that I already mentioned and maybe a few in Southold and Mattituck. And the majority of people here are very prejudiced. To tell you how bad prejudice is, the North Fork Country Club still doesn't seem to have any Jews or Italians on its membership list. So you can imagine the feelings about blacks. Actually, most white people here still say Negroes and coloreds. It a very backward area in a lot of ways. My mother says it's John Birch country. Anyway, Hank Allen is black and Maura was sitting very cozily with him and I guess that shocked a lot of kids. I have to admit that as sophisticated as I am about the black and white thing—I mean, growing up in New York in the Village, it's hard to be shocked by anything —I was a little surprised to see Maura with him. Only because we lived where we did.

"What do you think?" I asked Jeff.

"Personally, I don't give a damn who Maura goes out with and don't look at me like I have some secret crush on her or something because I don't. But I do like her . . . and it's not only social suicide for her to be seen with him but dangerous where the other blacks are concerned. Before you moved here some guy was seeing a black girl and he was beaten up pretty good."

"And how long ago was that?"

"You know as well as I do that things change very slowly around here."

I started to ask Jeff who beat up the guy but Stimpson blew her whistle and called for everybody in Scene 5 to come on stage. Maura and Hank stood up and walked toward the front. When she got to the bottom of the steps he leaned over and kissed her on the forehead and, believe me, the intake of breath in that theater could have been heard around the world. Maura pretended she didn't notice but I know she did. She smiled up at him—he towered over her —and they waved at each other and he left.

Janet came over and sat behind us. "What do you think of that?"

"Jeff says she's in for trouble."

"Well, this we know. But she's already had trouble from what I hear. Her family's hysterical about it and some of the black kids in school gave her a hard time this spring."

"How long's it been going on?"

"Three or four months. Didn't you know?"

I hadn't and neither had Jeff.

"Supposedly she's not seeing him anymore . . . at least that's what her family thinks . . . but I guess she is. He's super-looking, isn't he?"

Janet was one of the few who were not prejudiced. She was always helping minority groups and every-thing. Maybe it was because she felt like she was in a minority herself and, in fact, she was, I guess.

"I asked her to come with us tonight but she said

her parents won't let her stay out past eleven when she has to work the next day. But you know, I think she was really glad I asked her."

"Sure she was," Jeff said. "Why wouldn't she be?"

When rehearsal was over we were slowly getting ourselves together when Sue Rice ran in looking scared.

"Phil, Janet, you'd better come quick."

"What's wrong?" Janet asked as she started running for the door.

"It's Maura."

Jeff and I looked at each other and followed Janet. All I could think was that Stimpson and Hammand had already left and I hoped whatever it was wasn't too bad.

Outside, at the edge of the lawn, surrounding the front of the fence, were about twenty people. It was pretty dark so I couldn't see who they were, but as I got closer, I could see they were all black and they were all girls. Maura was facing them. Janet and Phil went running up on either side of Maura. One of the black girls, who was holding a big stick, spoke up.

"Now you just stay where you are, fatty . . . and you too, pretty boy."

"What do you want?" Phil asked.

"What we don't want is you buttin' in, whitey," another girl said. "Our business is with her."

Jeff and I walked up behind Maura.

One of the girls raised her stick. "Why don't all you good little kiddies get on home to your nice soft beddies, huh?"

"Just what is it you want?" Jeff asked.

"Who the hell are you?"

"I'm a friend of Maura's, that's who. What do you want?"

"Are you her old man or somethin'? Cause if you is, maybe there's somethin' you don't know." She took a step forward and we all backed up. It was really scary, all of them standing there looking so mad and carrying sticks.

"What's that?" Jeff asked. "What don't I know?"

"Maybe you don't know that your chick is seein' one of our guys, huh?"

"You mean Allen? Sure I know. He's a friend."

They all started laughing.

"He ain't no friend of yours, sweetie . . . he ain't no friend of no white boys. Maybe he like a little white chicken now and then, but he ain't no friend of no white boy."

"Maybe he's not as prejudiced as you are," Phil said.

"And you ain't prejudiced, huh, baby?"

"No, I'm not. None of us are. Why don't you come on in the theater and let's talk this thing over."

"We ain't got nothin' to talk over with you."

"Hey, man, let's get this over with."

"Who these dudes think they are, huh?"

"Let's teach that Harris bitch a lesson."

"Yeah, right on, baby."

Well, right then they started moving in on us and I don't know about Maura but I'd never been so scared in my life. We kept backing up and they kept coming.

"Listen," Maura said, "listen a minute, will you, huh?"

Everybody stopped moving.

"You got somethin' to say, white girl?"

"Yeah, I do."

"Well, spit it out between them white teeth a yours, honkie."

"Listen, you've got any beef it's with me, not them, so why don't you just let them all go?"

"We ain't stoppin' them. They can split any time they want."

Maura turned to us. "You'd better go," she said quietly.

"We're not leaving you here alone," Phil said.

"You don't understand," she said.

Jeff put his hand on her shoulder. "Yes, we do."

"We're not leaving you," Janet said.

Then Jeff walked over to the girl who seemed like she was the leader. "Look," he said, "if you're mad because Maura was seeing Allen, that's all over."

"Yeah, then what he doin' here tonight?"

"He came to see me," Jeff said.

"Oh, yeah, sure, man."

"He did—why don't you ask him?"

"What he want to see you for?"

"Because . . . because you were right, I *am* Maura's old man and we had to straighten a few things out, that's all. Anyway, that's between me and him. What's it got to do with you?"

"Listen, honkie, our chicks don't mess around with you guys . . . so why should your chicks mess around with ours, huh, tell me that, huh?"

"Why shouldn't everybody mess around with everybody?" Phil said.

"Oh, don't give us any a that white liberal crap, man. We ain't buyin.'"

"Okay, okay," Jeff said, "but whatever trouble you had with Maura is over, so why don't you go home?"

"How do we know that?"

"I'm telling you."

They started laughing again and in the distance I could hear the faint wail of a police siren.

"Why should we believe you?"

"Why not?" Phil asked.

"'Cause you is white liberal scum, that's why."

"C'mon, enough of this jazz, man, let's . . ."

"Hey, what's that?"

"Shut up."

The siren was getting louder.

"It's the fuzz, man . . . let's split."

"C'mon, man."

They dropped their sticks and started running down the street away from the approaching siren. The big one called back over her shoulder.

"We ain't through with you yet, Harris. We'll be seein' ya."

About fifteen seconds later the police car drove up. Two big cops, their guns drawn, jumped out.

"Okay, okay, break it up."

Well, we all started laughing. I mean, it was perfectly understandable why they'd think we were the riot, or whatever, because there were about twenty of us on the lawn at that point. I guess we started laughing out of tension or something but the trouble was we couldn't stop. The cops looked at each other.

"Hey, what's going on here?"

"Officer . . . we . . . we . . ." Phil started and then he doubled over with laughter which made the rest of us laugh even more.

"I think these kids are stoned, Joe," one said to the other.

And that made us laugh even more. Jeff fell on the ground and then Phil, Janet, and Walt went down.

"Hey, you kids, we're gonna take you in. Who made the call?"

"I . . . I . . . did," Mary El said, trying to stop her laughter.

"What's going on here?"

Finally, I stopped laughing and went over to the bigger of the two cops. "Look," I said, "I know how this looks but it's not what you think."

"Yeah, what is it then?"

"Well, there were some other kids here and they were threatening us and . . ." I started laughing again just remembering how scared I'd been.

"Threatening you? What the hell are you laughing for then?"

"Because we're scared," Maura said, squealing.

"They *must* be stoned," the big cop said.

"We gonna take them *all* in, Jack?"

"We gotta."

I guess we kind of sobered up when we heard that because one by one we stopped laughing. Janet was the first to start explaining and then we all joined in. The cops weren't too happy with us because we

couldn't (wouldn't) identify the kids who'd threat-
ened us. But none of us really wanted to start a war
with the black kids in Greenport. When the cops finally
left we closed the theater and six of us, including
Maura, went to the Apple Tree in Mattituck.

Actually, the Apple Tree was no longer the Apple
Tree. It had been renovated a month before and now
it was called the Coach House. But, as far as we could
see, the renovation consisted of a few new shingles
on the outside, a different roof, and some movie post-
ers inside. Sometimes we went there instead of Fisherman's for a change and, besides that, they served
later.

When we sat down we were six very shaken people.
The only thing we could possibly do was eat. Jeff and
I each ordered a bowl of spaghetti with sausages . . .
something we always had when we were nervous
or upset; and even Janet, who hardly ever ordered
anything when we went out, was having a hamburger.
After we gave our order we just kind of looked at
each other for a little bit until Jeff finally cut the silence.

"What I want to know is what you said to the police,
Mary El."

"I'm not even sure I remember. It was really gross.
I was so scared my knees were knocking together."

"That must have been some racket," I said.

"Thanks. Anyway, I think I said that there was . . .
you're not going to believe this . . ."

"I will," Jeff said.

"I said, 'You'd better come quick, there's an interna-
tional riot going on at the theater.'"

We all laughed.

"That's why they kept asking us what nationality we
were."

"I wondered about that," Phil said.

"I meant interracial," she said, jutting over her lower lip and looking like a big overgrown baby.

"This we guessed," Janet said. "Well, the point is you

got them there. It never occurred to me to call the police."

We all agreed that no one else had had the sense to think of that.

"Are you all right now, Maura?" Jeff asked.

"Sure. Listen, I'm really sorry I got you guys all mixed up in this."

We assured her that it was okay and then our food came.

"Are you going to stop seeing that guy?" Mary El asked.

It was a question we all wanted to ask, I guess, because everyone stopped eating and waited for Maura's answer.

"I guess I have to. Even though I don't want to. See, my parents brought me up to ignore stuff like color. My father's with the government and . . . well, we've lived all over the world. And when we moved here, I just didn't understand how things were. I didn't make any friends 'cause I guess I look snotty or something. . . . Anyway, when Hank started paying attention to me I started going out with him and everybody got real uptight about it, including my parents. At first I thought they were hypocrites, but I guess they knew what the situation would be here and they were scared for me. In school, the black girls used to bump me in the halls and stuff but nothing like tonight. I guess I don't blame them. But the white kids weren't any better. They gave me a hard time, too." She took a swallow of her Coke and, as she looked down the length of her straw, she added softly: "So that's why I don't have any friends."

We all kind of glanced at each other and then Phil said: "You do now, Maura."

Slowly she raised her head and shyly looked at each of us. "I know you all wanted Penny to get the part of Reno."

"Yes," I said, "that was true at first but, well, I, for one, can see now that as much as I love Pen, and as good as I think she is, you're better, Maura. You deserved the part."

"Hey, really?"

Everyone agreed.

For a minute I thought she might cry. "And Phil's right—we are your friends."

"Well, you sure acted like my friends tonight. It's been a long time since anybody took my part in anything." She glanced down at her watch. "Hey, I gotta get out of here. My parents are going to have a fit."

"I'll walk you to your car," Jeff said.

They both got up.

"Hey, listen, thanks again . . . for everything."

"I'll see you tomorrow," I said.

"Oh, right. . . . Weeeeeoooo," she said and they left.

When they were gone we discussed the fact that we'd been wrong about Maura and that she was okay and then Mary El and Janet got into a conversation and Phil turned to me.

"Some night," he said.

"Yeah."

"I was wondering . . . have you seen *Cabaret*? It's at the Greenport."

I had but, naturally, I said I hadn't.

"Would you like to go tomorrow night?"

There, he'd done it. He'd finally asked me out. Of course, I said yes. I told him where I lived and he said he'd pick me up at six thirty. Jeff came back and when I saw him walk through the door, my joy at Phil asking me out kind of faded.

On the way home Jeff and I talked about the events of the night and I kept debating with myself whether or not I should tell him about my date with Phil. When he stopped in front of my house I saw that I had no choice, because he said, "Should we go to the movies tomorrow night or what?"

"I can't," I said, putting my hand on the car handle for a quick getaway.

"How come?"

"I have a date . . . with Phil."

"Oh," he said.

I looked at him. He looked regular. "Is that all you're going to say?"

"What do you want me to say? Hallelujah?"

"I thought you'd be mad."

"No. I guess he's okay."

"Why don't you ask Maura and then we could double?"

"Why don't you mind your own?" he said, smiling.

"Sorry. Okay, well . . . I'll see you Sunday, I guess."

"Yeah. . . . Listen . . . I hope you have a nice time, really."

"Thanks."

As I walked to the door I thought that my premonitions about strange things to come had certainly been right. First the encounter with the black girls and now Jeff's complete turnabout. What next? When I opened the door I found out. My mother was standing in the hall, cigarette in one hand, drink in the other.

"Where the hell have you been?" she said angrily.

She never waited up for me and it was only eleven thirty—thirty minutes before I was supposed to turn into a pumpkin. What was going on?

"I want to talk to you," she said.

What next indeed!

Chapter 10

She walked into the living room and motioned me to sit down.

"Are you all right?"

"Sure," I said. What was she talking about?

"Do you want to tell me about it?"

"About what?"

"Please, Camilla, don't play dumb. I know all about it."

"Well, if you know all about it then why do I have to tell you anything?"

She looked at me a moment, her blue eyes taking on that glaze which she thought looked severe or authoritarian. Actually, I'd always thought it made her look nearsighted. She lit another cigarette.

"I want to know what happened at the theater tonight. Rachel told me that the police had to be called."

Rachel? I couldn't remember Rachel being there on the lawn.

"Were you arrested?" she asked.

"Of course not. Rachel wasn't even there," I said.

"Apparently she was . . . at least she was down the street, or something."

Obviously, Rachel had gone to Carvel after rehearsal with some of her ditsy friends and on the way home had seen the police cars. I hadn't intended to tell Mother about it, not because she was one of those mothers who would get hysterical and pull me out of the show or anything—at least I hadn't thought she was—but because she *would* worry. Now I had no choice . . . so I told her.

"That poor child," she said, when I had finished. "What a cruddy place this is. You can't blame the black girls, you know."

"I don't," I said. "I understand their position, but still I'm worried about Maura."

"I don't think they'd really do anything," Mother said. "They probably just want to scare her. I think you'd better tell Susan Stimpson what happened. She should stick around until all of you are out of the theater."

I agreed.

"Camilla," she said, looking into her glass and jiggling the ice cubes . . . a thing she always did when she wanted to tell me something important, "I *was* planning to go away for the weekend."

"Was?"

"Well, now it makes me a little nervous to leave you and Rachel alone."

"They're not after *me*, Mom."

"True. You're sure you'd be all right if I left?"

"Of course. Where're you going?"

"Stonington. Ray Fowler has a house there."

A weekend with Ray Fowler! So she *did* like him. I couldn't have been happier. Thrilled, I guess you could say. "That's neat."

"He's having a party . . . a lot of people will be there. He has a big house—a lot of people will be there for the whole weekend . . . staying there."

That little speech was, of course, to let me know that she wouldn't be alone with him in the house . . . so that I wouldn't think that she was sleeping with him. For an analyst, sometimes my mother is pretty dumb . . . and prudish or something. I mean, after all, she wasn't a kid and she *had* been married and how could she possibly believe I'd think that for all these years she'd been celibate. Anyway, I didn't want to embarrass her so I just nodded and said that it sounded like fun.

"I'll be leaving here around five A.M. so that I can get on the boat."

One of the big problems we have around here is the ferries to Connecticut. New London is right across the Sound from Orient Point and the ferry takes an hour and a half. But sometimes, in the summer, you can wait as long as eight hours to get on one if you're trying to take your car with you. It's really a disgusting situation.

"Why don't you go over on foot and have Ray pick you up?" I suggested.

"No, no . . . I'll get on that early one."

I knew why she wouldn't do it my way. If she did it that way then she'd be dependent on someone else. My mother is a very independent person . . . almost to a fault. Sometimes I think maybe her independence is what keeps her from marrying again.

Well, we'd better get to bed. You have to go to work in the morning, don't you?"

"Yeah . . . the WEO family awaits me."

She smiled and kissed me. "You don't *have* to work, you know."

"I like being independent," I said. "Of course, I'm not sure you'd understand that."

"Very funny. All right, darling, go to bed. I'll be back Sunday night about ten."

"Have a good time," I said and we hugged.

I started for the stairs and was at the bottom of them when she called my name. I waited for her to come into the hall.

"Cam," she said, "you *will* include Rachel in whatever you do tomorrow night, won't you? I don't want her to be alone in the house. I'm sure your friends won't mind if she goes to the drive-in or whatever."

It's hard to tell you what happened to me then. A million thoughts went through my mind at once. I couldn't tell her I had a date because she'd probably cancel her plans. And, of course, I couldn't take Rachel on the date but, at the same time, I was going to have to say that I'd take care of Rachel and . . . oh, God, what was I going to do?"

"Cam," she said, "did you hear me?"

I must have had a funny look on my face. "Yeah, I heard."

"Look, I know it's a drag to have a little sister around but it's just for one night . . . okay?"

"Okay."

As I climbed the stairs I had a very funny feeling in the pit of my stomach . . . actually, it was in my viscera, that's where you have feelings. While I was undressing for bed I kept trying to identify the feeling but I couldn't. The obvious was the dilemma I was facing but that wasn't what was bothering me—or rather, there was something else besides that.

I lay awake for a long time. And finally, it came to me. It had never occurred to my mother that I might have a date. It was true that I hadn't had an awful lot of dates in my lifetime, but I had had some and it didn't occur to her that I just might have one this particular Saturday. I mean, she didn't even ask. She just assumed that I'd be going out with the crowd. I guess it was kind of insulting. Obviously, my own mother assumed that I was a dud . . . a creep . . . a lame chick . . . a flop . . . an unwanted woman. It wasn't easy to take. I mean, was I such a disaster that even my own mother couldn't imagine the possibility of someone asking me out? Or was it just because she was so involved with her own plans that it didn't occur to her?

When I stopped feeling totally sorry for myself and realized that someone *had* asked me out, I was sure it was the latter. I felt better. But only for a second. Then I remembered I had the Rachel problem to deal with. What was I going to do? I refused to take her on my date. I mean, how would that look? It would be different if Jeff and I were doing something together but this was a *real* date . . . and I hardly knew him. What would he think if, when he arrived, Rachel came and jumped in the car? Would I have to break the date? As bad as that was, it was better than taking her along. What could I tell him? If I broke it, he'd probably never ask me out again. Should I tell him the truth? Knowing Phil even a little I was sure that if I told him the truth he'd insist on taking Rachel with us and if we did that someone was bound to see us and I'd be mortified. Maybe I could kill Rachel? Why couldn't she spend the night at one of her friends' houses? Why hadn't Mother thought of that? That's what Rachel usually did when Mother went away for a weekend. Obviously, they'd talked about that and it was no go for some reason. Maybe Rachel wouldn't mind staying alone? In fact, she'd probably love it. She'd have the television all to herself and . . . But Mother would hate it. I'd promised her I'd take care of Rachel. Of course, she'd never have to know. But *I'd* know. And Rachel would know and she'd use it to blackmail me at some later date. Maybe I could kill Rachel? Obviously, there was no way out . . . no solution. It was either breaking the date or killing Rachel and I'd feel too guilty if I killed her!

Without a doubt this was the worst thing that had ever happened to me. There was nothing I'd wanted more than a date with Phil Chrystie, and finally I'd gotten it and even Jeff had accepted it and now, because of my rotten, ugly, stupid, smelly, dirty, hateful, cretinous, idiotic sister, I'd have to give it up. Oh, why, why, why, wasn't I an only child? The thought of facing that repulsive person at breakfast almost made me throw up. I couldn't believe that on a night when I should have been glowing and lying in my bed unable to sleep for thoughts of the next night, I was lying there unable to sleep because the next night was going to be spent at home with that hideous creature . . . the bane of my existence . . . the scourge of my life . . . the epitome of horror . . . Rachel Crawford, the little sister. There was no doubt about it, I was born to suffer!

"What're ya lookin' at me like that for?" Rachel asked, hogging down some eggs I had made her.

"Don't talk with your mouth full."

She swallowed. "I repeat: What're ya lookin' at me like that for?"

"Like what?"

"Horrible."

The truth was I was wondering how come Rachel looked so much like a frog or a toad ... I wasn't sure which. I was also wondering how she could eat so much all the time and never gain an ounce. It was disgusting. If I so much as looked at a cookie I gained twelve pounds. My spaghetti-and-sausage madness the night before had puffed me up in less than twenty-four hours. Rachel buttered a piece of toast.

"What are you going to do today?" I asked.

"I dunno. Don't ya want your eggs?"

"No. I don't want my toast either."

"You shouldn't waste food," The Little Horror said.

"I'm sure you'll see that it doesn't go to waste."

"It's wrong to waste food when so many people are starving all over the world." She leaned over and took my plate and began digging into my cold eggs. "Cold," she said.

"Tell me something, Rachel: If I ate my eggs would those starving people be any less hungry?"

She looked at my dumbly. "Huh?"

"Never mind." The logic of eating everything that's put in front of you because of the starving children in China or wherever has never been something I could understand. "What are your plans for tonight?" I asked.

Again she looked at me dumbly, bacon clutched in her fingers which stopped halfway to her piglike mouth. "Whatever you're doin', I guess."

"Why aren't you staying with one of your friends?"

"I decided I didn't wanna." Her fangs snapped the bacon in two.

I couldn't believe what I'd just heard. "Rachel," I said carefully, trying not to reveal the venom stockpiling inside me, "you mean you could have stayed overnight at Sue's or Donna's or somebody's and you just decided you didn't feel like it?"

"Yeah."

I was speechless. This hideous little frog-toad that sat across the table from me, wiping up the egg from my plate with her fourth piece of toast, decided she just didn't *want* to stay with any of her friends, for God's sake! "WHY?" I shouted.

She pushed back her glasses with her paw. "What're ya shoutin' for?"

"Answer me, Rachel."

"I thought it would be more fun to hang out with you guys."

"Well, it's not going to be more fun." I stood up and grabbed her out of her chair. "You go to the phone right now and call one of those little beasts and tell them you're spending the night."

"Nope."

"What do you mean, nope?"

"I told Mommy I would stay with you and that's what I'm gonna do."

"Rachel," I said between my teeth, "you get on that phone."

"It's too late, Camilla. None of the mothers would let me stay without Mommy's permission."

"*I'm* giving you permission."

"Ha," she said. "Your permission doesn't count."

"You mean they won't let you stay unless Mommy says it's okay?"

"Right on, sister."

I hate that expression and Rachel knows it. "Rachel, what if I told you that I don't want you with me tonight?"

"What if you did?"

"I'm telling you."

"So what? You think that's news?" She sat back down and poured herself another glass of milk.

So she'd known all along that I wouldn't want her

with me and still The Hideous Weasel had forged ahead.

"What do you care if I come or not!" she said, her milk dripping onto her rat lips. "What's the difference? Do you all talk dirty or somethin' and you think you won't be able to with me around? I'm not a baby, ya know. I probably know more dirty words than you do. Wanna hear some?"

"No." Well, this was really something. I decided that if I couldn't keep my date the least I could do was to make The Snake feel guilty. "It so happens, Rachel, that I am *not* going out with the crowd tonight. It so happens that *I* have a date."

She looked at me for a moment, her hippo eyes blinking behind her enormous glasses, and then, as if someone had stuck a pin in her, she shrieked with laughter. In fact, she laughed so much and so hard that she rolled off her chair and onto the kitchen floor.

I could still hear her laughing when I got into Mrs. Ahlers' car.

"What's that funny sound?" Mrs. Ahlers asked.

"It's our pet monkey."

"What pet monkey."

"It's called Rachel."

Sam nodded and we drove off to our A&P WEO life.

The store was particularly horrible on Saturdays. Naturally it was packed with weekenders. And, as beastly as the week people were, the weekenders were worse. The only way I kept my sanity was to try and guess what kind of person stood above the order I was doing. I purposely wouldn't look at the person until I had finished ringing up. By the end of the summer I would be pretty good at it. But at this point, I could only guess one out of six or seven. Fat people were the easiest. Tons of ice cream, cake spaghetti, potatoes, and anything that had over a thousand calories a mouthful. You'd think they'd be embarrassed to buy all that stuff but they never were. When twelve o'clock came I looked for Maura to have lunch with, but Sam told me she'd gone home. Sam couldn't have lunch either because he had an analyst's appointment. So I decided I'd just walk around and try to think what to do about the night ahead. I knew I should have called Phil by now but I couldn't bring myself to. It was clear though that if I didn't come up with a solution by the end of my lunch hour, I'd have to call him.

When I got outside Janet and Mary El were waiting for me.

"What are you doing here?"

"We came to celebrate with you," Mary El said.

"Celebrate what?"

"Your date with Phil," Janet said, smiling.

Janet was the most fantastic friend a girl could have. I had been very nervous about her reaction, knowing how she felt about him, but with everything else that had happened, her feelings had slipped my mind. Now here she was, telling me she was happy for me.

"There's nothing to celebrate," I said. "I have to break the date."

"I have my car," Mary El said. "Let's go to Drossos."

Drossos was a restaurant-motel and what was, laughingly, known as an amusement center. The amusement center consisted of some Skee-Ball alleys, three pinball machines, a shooting gallery thing, and miniature golf. In the car I told them about my problem with The Dreadful Rachel.

"Gross," Mary El said.

"That's no problem," Janet said. "We'll take Rachel with us."

"You mean it?"

"Sure, why not?"

I threw my arms around her neck and kissed her. "You're the best friend I ever had. I can't believe it. I mean I thought you'd be all upset about my date and everything."

"Look, Cam," she said, "it's true that I'm madly in love with Chrystie but if I can't have him—and this we know . . . at least not while I'm in this condition—" She waved both hands over her body, indicating her weight. "—I can't think of anybody I'd rather see him involved with."

Well, it was all set. Phil would pick me up at six thirty and the kids would pick up Rachel at about seven. Surely The Iguana could be by herself for half an hour. Naturally, the afternoon went by very slowly. Finally, at five, I shot down the street to Sweet Bottom where I bought a super pair of rust-colored pants and a tan top with little rust-colored flowers on it.

When I got home I only had about forty-five minutes before Phil came. I told The Hyena, who laughed every time she looked at me, what the plans were and to make herself a sandwich or something.

"Aren't ya gonna eat?" she asked.

"I don't have time."

"Where ya goin' on this date?"

"To the movies."

"Are ya gonna make out in the back row?"

"Don't be disgusting. Go eat."

"What are the other kids gonna do—where are they gonna take me?"

"Look, Rachel, they are not *taking* you anywhere . . . you are being *allowed* to go with them, so get that straight right now. There's a difference. And you'd better not give Janet any trouble."

"Well, where are they going?"

"I don't know what their plans are. Now will you get out of here so I can shower, please."

"What are ya takin' a shower for? Is he gonna take your clothes off?"

"Get out!"

Rachel wasn't exactly the cleanest person in the world. It was hard for her to understand why anyone would just *want* to take a shower, because she never took one unless she was forced or unless even she could smell herself. I suppose it was a stage . . . but, fortunately, one that I had never gone through. Half the time when she was in the bathroom she just turned on the shower and sat on the john and read magazines. I know because she forgot to lock the door once and I walked in on her.

Phil arrived promptly at six thirty. Rachel got to the door before I did.

"Hi, Phil."

"Hi. Is your sister ready?"

I came down the stairs. "Hello, Phil."

"Hello, Camilla. You look very nice."

I smiled and then Rachel The Cretin said, "She took a shower and everything."

Naturally, that made it sound like it was a rare occasion and nobody knew what to say except, of course, for Rachel.

"How come you're going to see *Cabaret*? Cam and I saw it twice last year."

I thought I would die but Phil just smiled and said, "Anything worth seeing twice is worth seeing a third time, don't you think?"

Quickly, I hurried him out of the house after warning The Abominable Snowoman to behave herself.

In the car, as he started the motor, he turned to me. "We don't have to see *Cabaret*. I've seen it, too. We could do something else."

"I want to see it again."

"Good. So do I," he said and we started out of the driveway.

On the way to the movies we talked mostly about *Anything Goes* and I decided that even after that awful beginning it was going to be the most wonderful night of my life. Phil, it seemed, could handle anything.

could smell herself. I suppose it was a stage . . . but fortunately, and that I had never gone through that the same when she was in the bathroom she

Chapter 11

~~~~~~~~~~~~~~~~~~~~~~~~~~~~~~~

Since neither of us smoked, Phil bought orchestra seats and we sat downstairs. I was glad he'd done that for two reasons. One: I think making out in the movies is disgusting. . . . I mean, why should you subject other people to something so personal? Obviously Phil felt the same way or he would have bought loge seats. And two: He was thrifty and I like that in a person. There wasn't anyone in the audience that I knew and I was a little disappointed that nobody was there to see me with Phil. Actually, that wasn't quite true. Mr. and Mrs. Wetmore were there but he was about eighty-two and she was in her late seventies and I don't think they cared who I was with or if I was there at all.

Halfway through the movie Phil took my hand. It was really nice the way he held it. It wasn't too hard or too soft and it wasn't sweaty at all. When George Wilks had held my hand it was very sweaty and, naturally, kind of sticky. Because of George's personal hygiene problems at that time, whatever he'd been eating or touching on the day of the date was incorporated into the handhold. Usually, when I got home and looked at my hand, it was a dark grey even though it had started out perfectly clean. And Harlan Young was a cruncher. Whenever he'd take my hand he'd squeeze so hard that you could almost hear the bones crunch. I could certainly *feel* them

93

crunch. He also had to keep shifting positions, so that our hands were in constant motion. I often thought it was as though we were practicing to work with puppets or something. But Phil was perfect. Just the right amount of pressure and only three changes of position throughout—exactly at the right moment: immediately before my hand was about to go to sleep.

When the movie was over and we were back in the car he asked me if I was hungry. Now I hate girls who are golddiggers but I knew Phil had a good summer job and was making some money, and besides I was starving so I said yes. We decided to drive to Riverhead to the Neptune, which is an all-night diner. I was glad he wanted to go there rather than Fisherman's or the Apple Tree because I was pretty sure we wouldn't run into any of the crowd there at this hour. And I guessed that Phil had the same thought and it made me feel terrific that he wanted to be alone with me.

The Neptune, though it's really tacky inside, black-and-gold decor, has two very special features. Each booth has its own personal jukebox. In other words, you can play a song and hear it right at your table and if someone else plays something you hate you can turn it off. The second feature is the best bread pudding I've ever tasted. I ordered a cheeseburger, French fried onion rings, a Coke and, of course, bread pudding. Phil had the same except for the pudding.

He dropped a quarter in the slot and told me to play what I wanted. You get two plays for a quarter so I said I would play one and he should play the other. (My mother remembers when you got six plays for a quarter—that must have been neat.) Anyway, the reason I wanted him to play a song was because I think you can tell where a person's at by what song they pick. Also, sometimes a song can be a message, if you know what I mean. I played

"Dreamin' Again" by Jim Croce, which starts: "Don't you know I had a dream last night? And you were here with me. . . ." I watched for Phil's reaction to the song but he didn't seem to notice. Then the song he picked came on. Amazingly enough, he had also picked Jim Croce . . . but what he picked was "Bad, Bad Leroy Brown" and, try as I might, I just couldn't find a message for me in that particular song. Oh, well, at least we'd picked the same singer! Now that I look back on it I wonder if it was in any way prophetic that we'd both picked a singer who would die in a plane crash by mid-September?

On the way to the diner we'd talked about *Cabaret* and Liza Minnelli and Judy Garland, who Phil was crazy about. Actually, I'd never liked her too much but I thought maybe it was because my mother was always talking about her and playing her records. I'd always thought Garland was old-fashioned and square. But if Phil liked her, maybe there was something I'd missed. I'd have to listen again.

Before our food came we talked about how tacky the Neptune was and how most of the restaurants on the North Fork were basically tacky. Even the best ones were always ruined by plastic flowers and that awful fake wood they put on the walls because they thought it created a cozy quality. But, when our food came, Phil switched the conversation to Jeff. Suddenly, he was asking me tons of questions about him. Where was he born? Was he a good student? What were his interests? What were his parents like? On and on and on. I thought maybe he was asking me all that stuff because he thought Jeff and I were a couple, so I made it very clear just what our relationship was. Still, he kept asking me things about him. I didn't really mind because I liked Jeff and he was an interesting person to talk about, but then, when the conversation took a natural turn toward something else, he quickly brought it back to Jeff. For example:

ME: It must be wonderful to be in college. I wish I were going next year.

PHIL: You'll be there soon enough. What college is Jeff going to?

Or:

PHIL: I've always wanted a dog. My cousin had this sheepdog named Frogwell and when I was about twelve they mated him. My parents promised me a puppy from the litter but when they were born, well . . . they just said, no, a sheepdog was too much trouble.

ME: Why didn't you get something smaller?

PHIL: I wanted to. I saw a Yorkshire terrier in a pet shop I liked but my father said little dogs are for girls.

ME: That's crazy.

PHIL: I know. Does Jeff have any pets?

I tried changing the subject by asking Phil about himself.

"What are your parents like?" I asked.

"Oh, they're okay, I guess. My brother's the favorite though. Does Jeff have any brothers or sisters?"

You see what I mean? It always came back to Jeff.

"No. What do you mean, your brother's the favorite?"

"He just is. I'm the oldest and, I guess, not exactly what my father had in mind for a son. Jim my brother, likes to hunt and play ball and all that stuff and I never have. I guess you could say my brother is a sportsman. For instance my father hates that I'm into the theater thing."

"So does Jeff's," I said, and realized that now I'd done it.

It was ten thirty when we left the Neptune and I suggested that Phil come back to the house to listen to some Judy Garland records. I was sure that Rachel would still be out with the gang. On the way home I asked Phil what he wanted to do with his life.

"I'm not sure. I'm not a creative person and I don't like to work with my hands so I guess I'll go into some kind of business. Maybe banking. At least it's clean work."

Something about that made me feel very sad. Maybe it was the way he said it. He sounded particularly sad when he said he wasn't creative.

"Do you wish you *were* creative?" I asked.

"Sure. I think everybody wishes that secretly, don't. you?"

"Well, I know I do."

"But you are. You're a very good actress, Camilla."

"Do you really think so? Because, well, I hope to be a professional someday."

"It's a rough life, I hear."

"I know . . . but I think it's something I have to try. If I don't at least try it I'll never forgive myself."

"Do you think people should try everything they want even though it might . . . Oh, never mind."

"What? Ask me."

"I don't know how to put it," he said.

I could see that he was quite serious because his brow was very furrowed. "Go ahead, Phil—say what you were going to say."

"Well . . . I guess . . . Do you think a person should try things even though those things might not be acceptable to other people?"

"As long as it doesn't hurt other people. And I don't mean parents. I mean, some people have parents that want them to be one thing and they want to be another and if they end up doing what they want to do, instead of what their parents want, then their parents say that they're hurt. I don't think people should worry about that. Like Tina. Tina wants to be a minister—did you know that?"

"No, I didn't. That's interesting."

"But her parents want her to be a singer. It's kind

of unusual, isn't it? I mean you'd think it would be the other way around." He nodded. "Anyway, they say it's going to kill them, and all that kind of jazz, if Tina turns out to be a minister, and they don't really give a damn that it just might kill Tina if she can't be. You know what I mean? So that's not the kind of hurting I mean. If you want to do something that's going to make you happy and it doesn't hurt other people, why shouldn't you do it?"

"Even if society doesn't accept it?"

I couldn't imagine what he could be talking about. "What could you possibly do that society doesn't accept?"

He smiled. "There's plenty that society doesn't accept."

"Oh, you mean, like being a bum or something?"

"Well, I guess I wasn't just talking about a career. There are other things people want to do in life that have nothing to do with what you want to do for a living. I mean, well, society doesn't accept hippies and stuff like that."

"Do you want to be a hippie, Phil?" I couldn't imagine it. Not that Phil was a square but he just wasn't the hippie type.

"No," he laughed, "that was just an example. I wasn't thinking of anything in particular."

There was something about the way he said it that made me know there *was* something particular he was thinking of but he didn't want to tell me about it. Usually, I bugged people until they told but I felt I couldn't do that with him. Later that summer when everything began coming apart I remembered that conversation and I knew what he'd been thinking about.

"There *is* something I've always wanted to be," he said. "It's really stupid though."

"I bet it isn't."

"It's childish."

"Tell me anyway. I won't laugh. I promise."

"It's just a crazy fantasy. I could never really do it."

I waited and he glanced over at me when we stopped for the light in Cutchogue. I smiled encouragingly. The light changed and he looked back at the road. Neither of us said anything for about five blocks and then he cleared his throat.

"I've always wanted to be . . . a clown" he said. Then quickly: "You said you wouldn't laugh." And he laughed kind of way down in his throat.

Laugh? That was the last thing I wanted to do. What I wanted to do, and what I didn't dare do, was to cry. I mean if Walt had said that, or Penny, or even Sam, it would have been more understandable. But, Phil Chrystie? No way. Never had I met anyone less like a clown than Phil. How strange that he should want to be something obviously alien to him. "I don't think it's funny," I finally said.

"You don't?"

"No." Of course, I couldn't tell him what I really thought. "Why don't you do it if that's what you want?"

"Oh, I couldn't. It's just a childish fantasy. Anyway, I wouldn't know how to start."

"They have clown schools."

He shook his head. "No . . . I know it's not really for me. It's just something I like to dream about sometimes. Anyway, in all my life, I can't ever remember making anyone laugh."

I desperately wanted to tell him that that wasn't true—that he'd made me laugh hundreds of times—but I couldn't because it *was* true . . . or, at least, in my experience with him it was true. He was gentle and sweet and intelligent and certainly handsome, but one thing he wasn't was funny. He had never made me laugh nor had he ever made anyone else laugh in my presence. Keen wit and crazy antics were just not Phil's strong suit. I tried to picture him with a big red nose and floppy ears, wearing a checkered suit and doing pratfalls, but finally I had to stop because all it produced were tears in the corners of both eyes. I have a feeling he may have seen a similar image because I heard him swallow hard and then sniff. Neither of us said anything the rest of the way home.

We could hear the noise at least a block from my house. At first I thought it was coming from the public beach but, as we got closer, we could see all the cars parked in my driveway and along the side of the road.

"What's going on?" Phil asked.

"I don't know." I could feel fear creeping up me like poison ivy. Phil had to park in the public parking lot and we jumped out and started running toward my house. Some boys I'd never seen were leaning against a brightly painted Ford.

"Nothin' to run for," one of the boys said. "It's a drag, man."

We kept going. The door was open and before I stepped inside I could see that the hall and living room were filled with kids. The Allman Brothers were blasting on the stereo and a few kids were dancing but most of them were just standing around swigging from bottles of wine and, by the smell of the place, blowing dope. But the weirdest part of it was that I didn't see a single face I recognized.

"I don't know these kids," I whispered to Phil.

"You want me to call the police?" he asked.

"Yes . . . no . . . not yet . . . maybe our gang is here someplace." We pushed our way through a knot of kids and started toward the kitchen.

"Who ya pushin'?" a tall, tough-looking boy said to Phil.

"I'm looking for Rachel," he said politely.

"Rachel who?"

"Rachel Crawford. She lives here."

"I don't know no Rachel. Do you, Dave?"

"Never heard a her."

"C'mon," Phil said to me and took my hand as he led me through the pantry.

More unfamiliar faces were in the kitchen, although standing near the stove were two girls from a macramé class I took last year in Greenport. "Hey," I said, "what's going on here?"

The one who I think was called Diana looked at me blankly. "Hey . . . where do I know you from?" she asked.

"Macramé."

"Oh, yeah."

"What's happening?" I asked.

"I dunno . . . a party."

"Well, who's giving it?"

"I dunno. We were down at Kenny's Beach and a car full of kids came by and said there was this big party going on at Cedar Beach so we came. You bring anything to drink?"

"No. Do you know Janet Clark?"

"Janet Clark?"

"She's the fat one," her friend said.

"Oh yeah, the one who was crying," Diana said.

"What do you mean, crying?" Phil asked.

"Crying—you know, crying . . . boo-hoo."

"Where was she crying—when?" I broke in, impatiently.

Diana and her friend looked at each other, then shrugged as though they were Siamese twins. "I dunno," Diana said, "Earlier . . . in the living room. I don't know what it was about 'cause it was right when we came in. I think she ran upstairs or something."

"Let's go," Phil said.

We went back through the pantry, tripping over two kids who were sitting on the floor, their legs stretched across the doorway, and took the stairs two at a time.

"Janet," I called when I got to the top of the stairs. There were kids lining the hall. I looked in my mother's room and though kids were lying and sitting all over it, Janet wasn't among them. "Janet," I yelled again.

Then I saw Mary El's head poke out of my room. Phil and I ran down the hall. Janet was sitting in my rocking chair, tears streaming down her face. Mary El, Walt, Sam, and Penny were sitting around the room.

"Oh, God," Janet wailed. Then everyone started talking at once and I couldn't understand anything. I yelled at them to shut up and finally I got the story.

It seems that when they arrived to pick up Rachel, about ten of her creepy girlfriends were sitting around the living room playing records. Janet and the kids had planned to go to the drive-in but Rachel said she didn't want to go and why didn't they all stay and have a nice party? Janet tried to talk her out of it but, when Rachel wouldn't give in, they decided they'd better stay. Sam had wanted to come and get me at the movies but Mary El and Janet wouldn't let him. About an hour after they'd arrived, other kids started coming—kids none of them knew . . . not even Rachel. Sam and Walt told them they couldn't come in but they wouldn't listen and pushed in anyway. Before they knew it the house was filled with strange kids and there was nothing anybody could do. Janet had tried screaming them out but everyone had laughed and that's when she'd burst out crying and run up to my room. Apparently, what had happened was that Rachel had told her moron friends that she was having a party and the word had spread. It always does.

"Where is the little beast?" I asked.

Janet started crying again. For a moment I thought that maybe Rachel was dead or something and I started to panic and scream at Janet. When they calmed me down they told me that she wasn't dead . . . just dead drunk! Jeff was walking with her on the beach. Now the problem was what to do. How were we going to get these kids out of there without calling the police?

"Well, maybe we *should* call the police," Phil said.

"We'll all get busted," Walt said.

"This we know." Janet started to cry again. "Mrs.

Crawford will be called to the station on Monday. Oh, God . . . the ramifications are horrible."

"It's all so gross," said Mary El.

"Let's just tell them to leave," Phil said.

Sam and Walt looked at each other and smirked. "We tried that. They just laugh."

The door opened and Jeff entered, steering Rachel in front of him. "Here's the lush," he said.

I couldn't believe it. Both Rachel's eyes seemed to be going around in opposite circles and she had the most ridiculous smile on her face.

"Hello, Camel," she said.

I wanted to kill her. I guess it showed because, as I took a step toward her, Phil put a hand on my shoulder. "Rachel," I said, "what have you done?"

"Vomited," she said.

"Don't bother," Jeff said to me. "Save the lecture for tomorrow—she's out of it."

"Out of it, out of it, out of it," Rachel sang.

"I think we'd better put her to bed," Mary El suggested.

"Her rooms filled with kids," Penny said.

"I have to pee," Rachel said.

"Gross."

"I'll take her."

Penny took Rachel by both arms and guided her through the doorway and down the hall.

"Listen," Jeff said, "I think we've got to give it another try. Affectionate Al and my mother will be home from their bridge game soon and when they see all the commotion they'll be over here and then we're really in for it. Let's go down and try and get them out."

"What can we lose?" I said.

Sam said, "Teeth, and I've just gotten new caps."

"I think," Phil said, slowly, "I have a plan. Is everybody wearing a wristwatch?" We all were.

This was Phil's plan. He and Jeff would go down to the back porch, Janet and Sam to the living room, Mary El and Walt outside at the front of the house, and Penny and I would stay upstairs. Precisely five minutes from when we split we'd all start yelling, "Fuzz . . . Hey, it's the fuzz . . . Let's go . . ." and things like that. We all agreed it was a good plan.

We left the bedroom and when everyone else went downstairs I got into the bathroom with Penny and Rachel and told Penny the plan.

"Fuzz," Rachel said. "Fuzz. Fuzzy wuzzy wuz a . . ."

"Shut up, Rachel," I said, trying not to belt her.

Penny and I stared at our watches, silently.

"Boring, Rachel said. "I'm goin' downstairs."

"You're going nowhere."

One minute to go. I watched the second hand on my Mickey Mouse Electric creeping ever so slowly. Thirty seconds.

"I have to vomit," Rachel said.

"Go right ahead." Ten seconds. Whispering, Penny and I began the countdown together. Eight, seven, six, five, four, three, two, one . . . zero hour!

As Rachel started puking, I flung open the bathroom door and Penny and I began to yell. "Hey . . . It's the fuzz . . . Come on . . . Let's split . . . Fuzz . . . It's the FUZZ."

Downstairs, I could hear kids all through the house saying "Fuzz," and then the echo began upstairs and we heard running feet and the kids started pouring out of Mother's and Rachel's rooms.

A blonde girl stopped in front of me. "Hey, you better get moving—the fuzz is here."

"My sister's puking," I said.

She started down the steps. "Let her puke somewhere else," she yelled over her shoulder.

"I can't," I shouted at her back, "she's in love with this toilet." I wondered, if the blonde had heard me, would she remember it later and think I was crazy or what?

Kids ran past us and down the stairs and we heard shouts and cars starting up and, in the background, the sound of Rachel puking. At that moment, they were all wonderful sounds to my ears.

Well, Phil's plan had worked. Within ten minutes everyone but our crowd had gone. After Penny and I wiped Rachel off and put her to bed, we met the rest downstairs.

"I'm so sorry," Janet said. At first I thought she was apologizing again for the whole thing and then, when I looked around me, I realized what she was referring to, specifically. The house was a disaster area. Bottles, papers, cigarette butts, overturned furniture, broken glass, ashes ground into the rugs, and, worst of all, my mother's antique spinning wheel in pieces.

"Oh, no," I said, staring at it.

"Maybe I can put it together," Jeff said. Jeff was very good at carpentry but I didn't think even he could put this back together.

"I'll help you," Phil said. Later, I thought about Phil's offer and found it very curious.

"I think we'd better get out the old dustpan *now*. Really gross," Mary El said.

It took all of us about two hours to clean up the house and it was two A.M. before they left. Jeff and Phil planned to meet at my house at eleven thirty in the morning to fix the spinning wheel. Phil stayed behind when the others had gone.

"Well," I said, "I guess we'll have to listen to Judy Garland records another time."

"I guess," he said.

"Are you thirsty or anything?" I asked.

"No, thanks. I'd better get going. I'll see you tomorrow."

"Phil . . . I'm sorry."

"It wasn't your fault." He put his hand on the doorknob.

"Thanks for your plan. I don't know what we would have done if you hadn't thought of it."

He smiled shyly. "Somebody would have come up with something. Well . . ."

And then he took me very gently in his arms and kissed me. It was the most wonderful kiss I'd ever had. Not that I'd had millions or anything but I knew his kiss was the perfect kiss. Harlan Young was always shoving his tongue down my throat so I thought I would choke and George Wilks would always lick my teeth, which I never understood. Maybe it did something for George but it never did a thing for me. Phil's kiss was just right. Not too hard . . . not too soft . . . and it lasted just the perfect length of time.

"Good night, Camilla," he said. "I hope you have sweet dreams."

"Thank you. You too. And thank you for the movie and everything," I called after him as he was walking down the driveway. He waved his hand.

Before I went to bed I looked in on Rachel, who was snoring like some horrible old man. Tomorrow I would deal with her severely. I had no intention of telling Mother what had happened unless, of course, they couldn't fix the spinning wheel. And then it came to me. I remembered Phil's words: "I don't like to work with my hands." I'd heard it with my own ears. Why, then, did he offer to help Jeff with the spinning wheel? But, of course . . . there could only be one reason. If he came over to help it was an excuse to see me! Poor Phil. If only he'd known he didn't need an excuse. Now he was stuck with a project he'd hate and one he'd probably be no good at. I imagined him lying in bed, worrying about it. He was probably terrified he'd make a fool of himself in front of me when I saw that he didn't know how to use tools or anything. Well, I'd spare him that shame. While he and Jeff were working on the spinning wheel, I'd make myself scarce. Maybe he'd even realize what I was doing and he'd know what a sensitive person I was. What could be more romantic than a boy doing something he hated just so he could be near you? I was in heaven!

Chapter 12

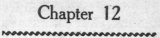

I stood against the doorframe of the poster-filled room my mother called her nightmare, staring at The Hideous Troll as she moaned and writhed in her bed. "Get up, Rachel. Eggs and toast and bacon and milk await you," I said.

"Ooooooh, noooooo," she groaned. Then she whispered: "Coke."

"Coke? Heavens no. You need protein . . . nice, firm yellow eggies and thick, not too crisp, bacon. Poor little tyke."

"Please, Cam," she grunted, "don't."

"Don't what, angel? I'm just trying to take care of you. You need food to make you strong again. How about some nice hot cereal? Nice oatmeal with heavy cream. How does that sound, hmmm?"

"Oooooh, noooooo. Don't."

"Ahhhh, poor little kidlet. You don't feel so good, huh?"

"Let me die . . . just let me die."

"Oh, I couldn't do that, pet. Mommy would never forgive me. Nope. I'm going to take good care of my baby sister. Now let's get up, Rachel . . . come on— up . . . up . . . up!" And I whipped the sheet off her lumpy little body.

"Cold," she mumbled.

"Don't be silly, Rachel, this is the first of July. Which reminds me—you can do Rabbit, Rabbit. Then you'll have good luck all month. Come, darling, let sister help you." I leaned over and yanked her to a sitting position.

"Oooooo, noooooo," she yelped.

"Okay—out of bed . . . at the end," I said. Rabbit, Rabbit is a game—well, not exactly a game, more like a superstitious thing you do on the first of every month. My Aunt Kate taught it to me when I was very little and I taught it to Rachel. In the morning, on the first, you have to get out of bed at the end, turn around to the right three times, and say "Rabbit, Rabbit" with each turn. Then you're supposed to have good luck for the whole month. Actually, I can't remember ever having had good luck for any full month. I had forgotten to do it myself that morning but now that I remembered it, I couldn't see why Rachel shouldn't have an opportunity for good luck . . . the little dear. "Move, Rachel."

"I don't wanna do Rabbit, Rabbit."

"You don't want good luck? Rachel, I think you're going to need it. Come on . . . out of bed."

She crawled to the end of the bed and let her legs slide over the edge until her toes touched the floor. Then, gradually, she pushed herself up to a standing position.

"Turn," I commanded.

She began to turn very slowly. "Rabbit, Rabbit," she said.

"Faster."

She turned faster. By the end of the third turn she was white and fell back on the bed.

"Oh, Rachel, you've ruined it. It doesn't count if you go back to bed. Now you'll have to do it all over again."

"I haven't gone back to bed," she said, grumpily. "I just fell *on* the bed. That's different."

"I can't see the difference."

"Well, I don't care, I'm not doing it again. I'm too weak . . . too sick . . . I may be dying for all you know."

"I find that hard to believe," I said, and left the room.

Jeff came over about quarter after eleven carrying his box of tools. He was bleary-eyed.

"I don't know, I just couldn't fall asleep," he said.

"Overstimulated," I said.

"What the hell does that mean?" he said testily.

Jeff was definitely in a mood. I shrugged my shoulders, indicating that it didn't mean anything in particular.

"Sorry." He started unpacking his tools. "What happened after we left last night?"

"What do you mean, what happened?"

"I mean, Camilla, what happened?"

"With Phil?"

He nodded.

"Nothing much. He kissed me."

"Oh."

It wasn't really unusual for Jeff to ask me what had happened on a date. It was the way he brought it up, then didn't ask for details, that was strange. Just "oh" and nothing more. That wasn't like Jeff at all.

Phil arrived while I was in the kitchen getting Cokes. When I came back to the front porch where Jeff was working on the spinning wheel, Phil was sitting on the floor next to him holding two broken pieces in his hands. He smiled at me and said hello and, when I asked him, said he'd like a Coke. After I got it, I excused myself and went back upstairs to find Rachel. As hard as it was going to be, I wasn't going to hang around and make Phil feel foolish.

Rachel was lying in the same position as when I'd left. Her eyes were closed and she looked like some horrible little gnome.

"Are you going to stay there all day?" I shouted.

She jumped. "Oooooh, noooooo."

"Sit up, Rachel. I want to talk to you."

"Please, not now."

"Now!"

Slowly, she raised herself to a sitting position and swung around so she was slumped against the wall. "Do we have to?"

"Yes." I waited. Rachel said nothing. "Well?"

"What?"

"Explain yourself."

"You won't believe me."

"Probably not," I said, "but try me anyway."

"I invited Donna over . . . that's all."

"You didn't ask anyone else?"

"Nobody."

"I find that hard to believe."

"You see, I told you."

"If the only person you invited was Donna, why were ten of your little friends here when Janet and the kids arrived?"

"Donna invited everybody."

"All right, maybe that's true—but what I want to know is why you invited Donna? You were supposed to be going out with my friends. You and you alone."

"So? You were supposed to be taking care of me and you didn't."

I could feel the threat of blackmail beginning around the edges. "I don't understand that logic, Rachel."

"You changed your plans, I changed mine."

"I didn't exactly *change* my plans. I never *planned* to spend Saturday night with you. That little plan was imposed on me. Anyway, the point is, Rachel, that you screwed up . . . dreadfully. And on top of everything you got drunk. Rachel, you're only fourteen years old."

"Fourteen and two months."

"That is still three years and ten months away from being able to drink legally."

"Nobody drinks legally."

"I don't care what nobody does," I said, "you're not nobody." My God, I thought, I sound just like my Mother . . . except it was usually I don't care what *everybody* does—you're not *everybody*. Somehow that sounded better than the nobody rap. Oh, well. I went on: "What did you drink?"

"Blackberry brandy." She swallowed and the little color there was went out of her cheeks.

"Who gave it to you?"

"Kurt Binns."

"Kurt Binns? He's your age, isn't he?" Besides that, he was the son of one of our most prominent ministers. "Where'd he get blackberry brandy?"

"Do you have to keep sayin' it?"

"Saying what?"

"BB."

"Blackberry brandy?"

"Oh, please, don't say it again."

"Where'd he get it?"

"He stole it from his father's liquor cabinet. What difference does it make?"

"How much did you drink?"

"We split the bottle . . . it was a pretty big bottle. I think I'm gonna be sick again."

"No, you're not. Just stay where you are. Rachel, I don't remember seeing Kurt here."

"Well, he was here."

"The point is you screwed up."

"You said that."

"Well, what are you going to do about it?"

"What can I do now? It's over."

"You can pay," I said.

"Huh?"

"I'm not planning to tell Mommy unless they can't fix the spinning wheel."

"What spinning wheel?"

"*The* spinning wheel. Your friends broke it and Phil and Jeff are downstairs right now trying to put it back together. If they can't I'll have to tell Mother what happened."

"And if they can?" she asked, becoming a little bit more alert.

"Then you and I will work something out."

"Oh, yeah? What, for instance?"

"I'm not sure yet."

"Well," she said, crawling off the bed and looking for her slippers, "what we'll work out is that I won't tell Mommy that you left me all alone and you won't tell

Mommy . . ." She smiled suddenly. "As a matter of fact, you won't tell Mommy anythin' because if you tell her what happened then you'll automatically be tellin' her that you left me alone."

. "I didn't leave you alone, Rachel . . . I made provisions for you." I knew she'd pull something vile.

"You left me alone for half an hour."

"You are a disgusting slime," I said. "You act as though you've never been left alone in your life."

"Not when Mommy has asked you to watch out for me I haven't." She put on her glasses and her beady eyes narrowed to tiny little pinpoints. "I think," she said, "the less said to Mommy, the better."

"And what about the spinning wheel? What do we say about that if they can't fix it?"

She opened her mouth to say something but never got a chance because Jeff yelled for me to come downstairs—quick.

"We'll settle this later," I said as I left the room.

"Out here," Jeff said.

I hurried out to the porch. "Oh, my God," I said. There, slumped against the screen door, was Kurt Binns. He was a mess. Vomit was crusted on his shirt and his hands and face were filthy.

"Hi," he said. "I just woke up."

"He slept on the beach," Phil said.

"Your mother and father must be frantic."

"I'm never going home," he said. "Anyway, I promised to marry Rachel last night."

I was beginning to feel as though I was in the middle of some ridiculous French farce. "Rachel is in no condition to marry anyone," I said, "and from the look of it, neither are you."

"I could take a shower," he said.

"Yes, well, she couldn't!" Only I could appreciate the humor in that.

"Do you want to call your parents?" Jeff asked.

"No."

"Kurt, you have to go home sometime."

"Why?"

We all looked at each other.

"They'll beat me," he said. "They'll tie me to a post in the cellar and beat me with rubber hoses and then they'll put electrodes on my head . . ."

"Kurt," I said, "I know your parents."

". . . and then they'll stick slivers under my nails and drip water on my forehead and . . ."

"You have to go home," Jeff said. "You want me to drive you?"

"You don't believe me, do you?" he asked.

"No." We spoke in unison.

"What'll I tell them?"

"Anything but the truth," I said. "I mean, you can't say you were here and got drunk. You'll get me in trouble and since I didn't have anything to do with it, I don't think that's fair."

He nodded. "I could say I was kidnaped."

"I don't think that would go over," Phil said.

Suddenly Kurt smiled, a strange light coming into his large brown eyes. Then he took off his shirt, rolled it into a ball, and handed it to me. "Would you mind throwing this away?"

"Sure. What is it? What did you think of?"

"Don't worry," he said, his smile growing, "I won't involve any of you."

"You want me to drive you home?" Jeff asked again.

"Oh, no . . . that wouldn't fit in with my plan." He opened the screen door and went down the steps. Then he faced the water, his arms stretched upward. "God," he yelled, "I've found God. . . . I've spent the whole night with God!" And he began to run toward the water. Then he stopped suddenly, turned, and yelled back at me. "Tell Rachel I'm sorry I couldn't marry her today but something came up!" He started toward the water again, his high squeaky laughter trailing behind him. When he got to the water's edge he turned left and started running along the beach toward Southold, where he lived. We watched silently until he was out of sight.

"I think he's still drunk," Jeff said.

"I sure would like to see Reverend Binns's face when his son comes racing in, smelling like a bar and screaming that he's spent the night with God."

"I think it's damn clever," Jeff said. "He's picked the one thing it'll be hard for his father to argue about."

"I know Jack Binns pretty well," Phil said. "He'll never buy it. But don't worry, Camilla, I think Kurt will just say he took the bottle and went off by himself. He's a good kid—he won't want to get anyone else in trouble."

"Yeah, I think you're right." I looked at the spinning wheel for the first time since I'd come back to the porch. It seemed to be in more pieces than when they had started. Maybe I could tell Mother God had visited us and turned out to be a little clumsy!

Jeff saw the look on my face. "Don't worry, Cam ... we'll fix it."

I nodded and smiled encouragement before I went off again, leaving them to their work.

It was four o'clock when they called me onto the porch. Well ... you wouldn't say no one would ever notice, and you wouldn't say it was expert craftsmanship. What you would say was, someone had broken the spinning wheel and someone had *tried* to put it back together again. The first thing that went through my mind was to burn down the house so Mother would never know!

"I'm sorry," Jeff said. "It's the best we could do."

"I know. It's ... it's ..."

"It stinks," Jeff said.

"Do you think she'd notice if you just threw it out?" Phil asked.

"It's one hundred and fifty years old. I can't do that."

"She's coming home late tonight, isn't she?" asked Jeff.

I nodded.

"Well, she probably won't go in the living room.
. . . I mean, she'll probably just go to bed. Then
tomorrow she has patients and Tuesday she goes to
New York for two days, so maybe she won't notice."

"But she'll notice someday, won't she?" I asked,
hoping they could convince me that she'd never notice.

"Yes, but when she finally does, you can just say
you don't know anything about it . . . that it was there
the last time you looked."

"I don't know," I said.

"I have a plan," Phil said. "A plan that will leave
you basically innocent. Go upstairs," he said.

"Upstairs?"

"Yes. Go upstairs and don't come down for fifteen
minutes. Lie on your bed and don't move no matter
what."

Remembering how good Phil's last plan was, I did
what I was told. I lay on my bed and played some
Carly Simon. When the fifteen minutes were up I
went downstairs. They were gone and so was the
spinning wheel. A note was on the floor where the
spinning wheel had been.

TO WHOM IT MAY CONCERN:

If you wish to have your spinning wheel returned
then you must pay a ransom. We will be in touch
with you. Stay by your phone.

Well, frankly, I couldn't see how this left me basically innocent. I mean, I *did* know who took it, didn't
I? But, of course, I didn't know *where* it was—maybe
that's what Phil had meant. If Mother asked me if I
knew where the spinning wheel was I could honestly
say no. But what if Mother took the note to the police?
And what if the printing was traced? And what if
the whole thing was discovered and Phil and Jeff
were arrested and sent to jail? The whole thing was
too hideous to contemplate. I decided there and then
that when they came back I would tell them to bring

the spinning wheel back and Rachel and I would just have to take our medicine. But they never did come back. Hour after hour passed and finally, right before *The FBI* went on, I called Jeff's house.

"Hel-lo!" It was the Dragon Lady.

"Hello, Mrs. Grathwohl. Is Jeff there?"

"Who is calling, please?"

She knew very well who was calling, the old witch. I must have spoken to her a million times over the phone. I had to fight with myself not to say: "It is Raquel Welch, Mrs. Grathwohl, and I want to take Jeff away with me and make love to him until his head falls off!" Instead I said: "It's me—Camilla."

"Oh . . . yes?"

I was surprised she didn't ask Camilla who. "Is Jeff there?" I repeated.

"No, dear, he's not. He's gone out with his friend."

The implication, of course, was that I was *not* his friend. "Do you have any idea where they went?"

"I don't pry, dear . . . and neither should you."

The hell she didn't! I almost started to explain that I'd been expecting them back, but I didn't want to give the D.L. the satisfaction that I had been, in effect, stood up. "Well, would you tell Jeff that I called, please?"

"Certainly." Click.

The D.L. never said goodbye and I never got used to it. I slammed down the phone, as always . . . a futile gesture since she had hung up first.

I went upstairs to the study and joined Rachel in front of the television. It was a rerun I had already seen so I didn't pay too much attention. If the D.L. said that Jeff had gone out with his friend that meant that Jeff had probably taken Phil back to his house with him . . . which meant that the spinning-wheel caper had gone all right. They had hidden it somewhere and then gone back to Jeff's house. And then they had gone out again . . . without me! I couldn't figure that part out. They must know I'd be waiting.

Just then the phone rang. I motioned to Rachel to lower the volume.

"Can't ya take it someplace else?" she whined.

"Hello," I said.

It was Jeff. "Everything is cool . . . you know what I mean?"

"Yes. Where are you?"

"I'm home. I'm going to bed early . . . it's been *some* weekend."

"Oh, well, when did you get home?"

"I've *been* home," he said. "After we took care of you-know-what, Phil went home and I came home. I would have called earlier but Affectionate Al and my mother kind of cornered me and then there was dinner and . . ."

"It's all right, you don't have to explain." I wanted desperately to get off the phone. "I'll see you tomorrow—you'll pick me up for rehearsal?"

"Sure. Seven fifteen. Well, I hope it all works out. Good night."

I hung up, feeling sick to my stomach.

"What's wrong with you?" Rachel asked. "You look like you're going to puke."

"Acid indigestion," I said.

"It's your fabulous cooking."

"Probably," I said. I walked down the hall to my room and, after a few dazed moments, found myself sitting in my rocker staring out at the trees. If the D.L. was telling the truth, and I was sure she was because she always called him to the phone when he was home and awake, then Jeff had been lying to me. But why? Obviously, he had called from a phone booth, or somewhere other than his house, and he was with Phil. Why wouldn't they want me with them? There could be only one reason. They were going out to pick up girls! I'd never known Jeff to do that but Phil was a year older and maybe that's what he liked to do and he had persuaded Jeff to do it with him. How things changed in less than two weeks! That's why you could never count on anything . . . or plan anything. My mother was always telling me to try not to write the script and she was right. Ten days ago if anyone had told me that Jeff would have preferred spending an evening with Phil Chrystie instead of me, I would have said that person was crazy!

Well, maybe the experience would be good for Jeff. But I sure didn't like the idea of Phil out there picking up girls. Besides, picking up girls was a sexist thing to do. Of course, Phil owed me nothing. I mean nothing had happened between us except a kiss . . . and a few moments of sharing secrets . . . and a few adventures . . . and, oh, God, it seemed like a lifetime. I couldn't stand it. Why did he contrive to come over to help with the spinning wheel when he hated working with his hands just so he could see me and then run off with Jeff to pick up girls and not even call me or anything? Maybe they weren't picking up girls! But what else? Maybe it was a surprise for me? Who are you kidding? No way. Whatever it was, I was sure I'd find out sooner or later. Jeff could never keep a secret from me for very long.

Suddenly, I was sure I knew what it was. Phil was going to take Jeff somewhere to lose his virginity. Only *I* knew that Jeff was still a virgin. Everyone thought that he and Tina had made it but I knew the truth. They had tried but Jeff couldn't. He felt awful about it but I told him that that happened to lots of boys the first time and not to worry about it. So that was probably it. Jeff and Phil had gotten to talking and Jeff had told Phil the truth. Phil was definitely the kind of person you would tell the truth to—and Phil, being a kind and helpful type, had decided to take Jeff someplace, or to someone, and help him work the whole thing out. Of course, that was it.

Again and again, I convinced myself that Phil was saving Jeff from a life of celibacy and, again and again, some nameless, nagging thing told me that wasn't it. I was no closer to any real answers two hours later when I heard my mother's car in the driveway. I jumped up and ran into the study.

"Come on, Rachel," I said. "Mommy's home. We have to go into our act."

"There's something about this that seems fishy," she said.

"Well, you better make it good, because if it doesn't work . . ."

"Yeah, yeah, I know, we'll all be goin' to AA. Ready when you are."

The front door opened, Rachel and I counted to three and then went running down the steps.

"Mommy . . . Mommy . . . the spinning wheel . . . the spinning wheel's been kidnaped!"

She looked at us like we were crazy. Who could blame her?

Needless to say, Mother did not believe the kidnap story. So, naturally, the truth had to be told. I didn't mention Rachel's drunkenness because that really didn't have anything to do with the spinning wheel, or anything else, and Rachel was marvelous, for her, and tried to take the blame for everything. But Mother was mad at me for not doing what she'd asked me and said I couldn't go to any parties on the Fourth of July, which was Wednesday. Later, though, she came to my room and amended that.

She sat on the edge of my bed. "Why didn't you tell me you had a date?"

"Because I was afraid you wouldn't go on *your* date," I said.

She smiled and took my hand. "I'm sorry I didn't consider what your plans were. Sometimes I forget that you're growing up. I guess we were all wrong," she said.

"I'm really sorry about the spinning wheel."

"Well, tomorrow you can ask Jeff to bring it back and we'll forget about the whole thing."

"You won't like the way it looks."

"It's just a thing. Did you have a good time with ... what's his name?"

"Phil Chrystie. Yes, I had a great time until I got home."

"Do you like him a lot?"

"Yes. Very much. He's older, you know."

"How much older?"

"He's eighteen or nineteen."

"Oh."

"Did *you* have a good time?" I asked.

"Yes ... very."

"Do you like him a lot?"

"Ray? Yes ... very much," she said quietly.

We sat that way, me in my bed and Mother on the edge, holding my hand, and said nothing for quite a while. There wasn't anything uncomfortable or awkward in the silence and I don't think I'd ever felt closer to her. I knew she felt that way, too. Then she said:

"Ray is coming over for the Fourth. Maybe you'd like to invite Phil to join us for a barbecue."

"I'd like that very much. You'll like him. He's not anything like Harlan or George. I mean, he's a real person—do you know what I mean?"

"Yes, I think I do. How do you feel about Ray coming here?"

"I feel fine. I liked him."

"Good."

We were silent again and then she leaned over and kissed me on the forehead.

"I love you, Camilla," she said.

"I love you too, Mommy."

She squeezed my hand and quietly left.

It was a lovely time and one I knew I would remember always.

Chapter 13

~~~~~~~~~~~~~~~~~~~~~~~~~~~~~~

Jeff returned the spinning wheel when he came to pick me up and for a moment I thought Mother was going to cry. But instead, she started laughing and said that it looked like the largest jigsaw puzzle in history. Jeff, of course, informed her that the largest jigsaw puzzle in history had 10,400 pieces and measured 15 feet by 10 feet.

On the way to the theater Jeff acted as if nothing had happened. But, of course, he had no way of knowing that *I* knew *something* had. It was obvious that the D.L. had never bothered to tell him I'd called. Then, right before we got out of the car, he asked me if I could ride home with someone else because he wasn't going directly home after rehearsal. The way he said it, I knew that it would be useless to ask him what he was going to do, so I just nodded.

Eben made a short speech before rehearsal started, asking for volunteers to help with the set on Saturday and Sunday. I volunteered for Sunday. We blocked a scene and then took a break. This was when I planned to invite Phil to the barbecue. But when I looked around for him, I saw that he was sitting in the back of the theater with Jeff. They were deeply engrossed in conversation and something made me feel I shouldn't interrupt. Besides, I didn't want to invite him in front of Jeff. I guess I looked upset or something because right then I felt a hand on my shoulder.

"What's happening, Camilla?" It was Eben.

I was surprised because he'd never really talked to me before. "Not much," I answered.

"You look strung out."

"I do?"

"Yeah. I hear you had some deal at your house Saturday night. Sorry I wasn't there but . . . ah . . . I was busy." He gave me a big wink. I knew that he'd had a date with Tina and I thought the wink was piggy. He went on: "I could have gotten those slobs out of there in one second flat."

Though I'd never talked privately with Eben I'd been in group conversations with him and I knew he had an answer for everything. According to Eben, there was nothing he couldn't do. Stimpson was always telling him he was overextending himself but he'd shake his head and say, nah, he had plenty of energy and not to worry, he'd take care of everything. As it stood now, he was planning to build the set, do the lighting, help with props, and play the leading role. And as it turned out we ended up with a nice but sparse set because Eben never could get it together. Anyway, it didn't surprise me that he thought he could have handled the situation at my house. I just wondered *how* he thought he would have managed it.

"What would you have done?"

"Oh, I have my ways," he said and gave me another big wink and walked off.

There was something about Eben I didn't trust. Well, I guess it wasn't exactly that I didn't trust him. I just thought he was really, at the heart of things, quite inadequate and so he put on this big act all the time. I was amazed Tina had fallen for him because he was a much bigger clown than Walt. Of course, he was also much better looking—fortunately, not my type. I was sure he had lots of girls and I would hate to be involved with someone like Eben. He was slick . . . I guess that's the best way to describe him. A smooth operator, definitely not my type. Not that he'd shown any interest in me—but if he had . . . well, who knows what I would do. Anyway, I was glad things were as they were: Eben and Tina, me and Phil. I had to laugh at myself. Me and Phil! One date and I was making us a couple. I turned toward where Jeff and Phil had been sitting. Phil was alone. Quickly I walked to the back and sat down next to him.

"Hi," he said. "I heard about the spinning wheel. Your mother sounds like a terrific person . . . I mean, the way she took it and everything."

"She's pretty neat." I wished that I could have just rapped a bit before I gave him the invitation but the break was almost over and I didn't know how soon Jeff might be back. So, I blurted it out. "Phil, we're having a barbecue on the Fourth and I wondered if you'd like to come?"

"Ahhh, a barbecue? Who? I mean, who's having it?"

"My family."

"Oh . . . well . . . yes, sure, that would be nice. Thank you."

"What would be nice?" It was Jeff leaning in between us.

"Nothing," I said quickly. Phil looked at me curiously, then at Jeff, then back to me. I tried to make a joke of it. "Jeff Grathwohl, you are the nosiest person alive. You're going to end up just like Pinocchio."

"For your information, Camilla, Pinocchio got his long nose by lying, not by being nosy." And he walked away in a huff.

"Sometimes Jeff is just too sensitive to live," I said.

"Aren't you inviting him?" Phil asked.

He said it in such a way that I felt terribly guilty that I wasn't intending to invite Jeff. But, in my mind, it was not going to be that kind of barbecue. Mother was having Ray and I was having Phil. Who would Jeff be there for? Rachel? "Well, it's not that kind of barbecue," I said.

"What kind is it?"

I realized how awful that must have sounded. "I mean, I'm not having all the gang or anything."

Phil nodded as though he understood but I could see that he really didn't. Then Stimpson blew her whistle and rehearsal began again. I wasn't in the next scene so I stayed where I was while Phil excused himself and went to sit next to Stimpson. It hadn't occurred to me that Jeff might be hurt if I didn't invite him. Or had it? I realized that I didn't want Jeff there with Phil . . . but what I didn't understand was why. Anyway, Mother hadn't said anything about inviting Jeff and it *was* her barbecue, wasn't it? Of course, deep down I knew that if I asked Mother to invite Jeff she would have been more than happy to. She was very fond of him, and, actually, wouldn't think of leaving him out. I had just about decided that I was being horrible and that I would invite Jeff and tell him to bring a date when Janet came over and told me that Eben was having a Fourth party.

"I'm having my own with Mother," I said.

"Oh. Well, I'm sure you can get out of that, can't you?"

"I don't want to get out of it. Phil's coming."

"Ohhh . . . I see. Just you and your mother and Phil?"

"No. Mother's having a friend. And I suppose the baby sister will be there with one of her hideous friends."

"Well, that should be cozy. Are you and Phil a thing now?"

"No. Don't be ridiculous. Listen, can Mary El give me a ride home?"

"Sure. Where's Jeff going?"

I shrugged my shoulders. Secretly, I had been hoping that Phil would want to take me home but since he hadn't asked in the break he probably wasn't going to.

"You know," Janet said, "something weird is going on."

"Like what?"

"I don't know . . . but I'm getting vibes."

"Oh, you're always getting vibes."

"And?" she asked, raising one eyebrow—a thing I would have given my whole record collection to be able to do.

"And you're usually right," I said. Nine times out of ten she was. "What exactly do you feel is weird?"

"For one thing, Jeff is going somewhere tonight and you don't know where. That's very weird. Or maybe you do and you just don't want to tell me, huh?"

"No, I really don't. To tell you the truth he's been acting very peculiar the last few days." And then I told her what had happened the night before and how Jeff had lied to me.

"Mmmm," she said. "Got any ideas?"

I said no because I wanted to see what she came up with.

"I'll tell you this," Janet said, "if Chrystie is interested in any other girl besides you it's none of us. This we know."

"Maybe there's somebody none of us knows about."

"Could be—but somehow I doubt it. Don't ask me why because I don't know . . . its' just a feeling. Do you think Jeff is going somewhere with Phil again?"

"Maybe."

"Don't move," she said. "Janet Clark, girl detective, is about to find out."

I watched her go down the aisle and sit next to Mary El. They whispered for a few minutes and then Mary El got up and went over and sat next to Phil. She waited until Stimpson jumped up on the stage to talk to one of the kids and then she spoke to Phil. When Stimpson came back to her seat Mary El went back to hers and whispered to Janet. Then Janet waited a few minutes and came back to me.

"Get this," she said. "Mary El asked Chrystie if he

wanted to go to Fisherman's with us and he said that he couldn't."

"Did he say why?"

"She said that the way he said it she didn't dare ask him."

Exactly the way I had felt with Jeff.

"They're up to something. I've got an idea," she said and was on her way back to Mary El before I could ask her what it was.

About two minutes later it was time for one of my scenes so I didn't have a chance to talk to Janet until rehearsal was over. By then everything was arranged. Janet, Mary El, Sam, and I would follow Jeff in Mary El's car and Eben, Tina, Penny, and Walt, in Eben's car, would follow Phil.

"But they'll recognize the cars," I said.

"We'll stay far enough behind—don't worry."

"I once got Jeff to follow Linda for a whole night," Sam said. "It was awful. I saw that creep kiss her and everything. Anyway, she never knew we were following her."

"But Linda didn't know Jeff's car, did she?"

"That's true."

"Don't worry; at least we're not using the Silver Bullet," Janet said as she pushed me into the back seat.

"If Jeff ever found out he'd kill me."

"He won't."

"I think this is neat," Sam said.

"Me too," Mary El said, smiling at Sam. Sam moved over as close to the door as he could get.

"Let's get going."

"But Jeff hasn't even gotten into his car yet."

"We're going to wait near the train station; he's bound to come that way."

In about two minutes we saw Jeff's car go by. Mary El started up and pulled out.

"Don't stay too close," Sam said.

A part of me was very excited. The other part felt

awful. I knew I really didn't have any right to be following Jeff. After all, he had the right to some privacy and if he was doing something he didn't want me to know about . . . well, that was his privilege. I mean, we weren't joined at the hip, were we? But it was an adventure and it was exciting. I felt like we were in *Casablanca* and I was Ingrid Bergman.

We followed Jeff to Route 25, where he turned left and headed east. We stayed far enough behind so that he couldn't possibly know whose car it was in the dark. At South Harbor Road he turned. Mary El slowed down a little, then turned too. Jeff was quite far ahead.

"Maybe he's just going home," I said. This was the way to our houses.

"If he's going home, why didn't he take you?" Janet asked.

I slunk further down in the seat. He didn't take the left turn at Baywater Avenue he'd have to take to go home, but kept going on South Harbor. We all knew it was a dead end and a make-out place. Suddenly, Jeff's blinker started indicating that he was going to turn even though there was no right turn. Then he pulled over to the side of the road and stopped.

"What should I do?" Mary El screamed.

"Keep going . . . keep going."

"Go past him. Don't slow down."

We all ducked down in our seats except, of course, for Mary El.

"Really gross," she muttered, shooting past him. "Now he'll think I'm following him alone."

"He couldn't see you in the dark," Sam said.

"Then how come you all disappeared?"

"Never mind," Sam said when we got to the end of the road. "Turn around and go back."

"What if he's still there?"

"I hope he is. Go on—turn around."

When we got back to the spot where Jeff had pulled off he was gone.

"Now what?"

"We've lost him."

"Go down Baywater and turn into Bayview."

Mary El did and we went up and down lots of roads off Bayview but saw nothing. After half an hour, we decided it was a lost cause and went to Fisherman's where we had planned to meet the others.

They were already at a table when we got there.

"We lost him," Walt said. "Eben turned chicken."

"The hell I did," Eben said. "What did you expect me to do? I mean, the creep pulled off to the side of the road . . . I had to go past, didn't I?"

Our group looked at each other.

"Well," Janet said, "this is interesting. Jeff did the same thing. What direction did Phil go in?"

"He went up to Soundview Avenue and then over to Lighthouse Road. That's where he pulled over. I had to keep going so I jogged over to Young's, doubled around, and when we got back where he'd pulled over, he was gone."

"We combed Soundview and even went to Kenny's Beach but he wasn't there. You know who *was* there?" Penny asked, not waiting for an answer. "Bruce McDonald with Debbie . . . parked."

"Oh, who the hell cares about that?" Eben said. "The creep got away. That's all that counts. Man, I've never lost anybody before."

"Well, you sure lost this one, Sherlock," Walt said, turning the knife. I guess losing Tina to Eben bothered him more than he wanted to let on. Eben gave Walt one of his hard looks.

"Do you think they knew we were going to follow them?" Mary El asked.

"Obviously, they knew something," Janet said.

"Maybe they weren't even meeting each other. I mean, if they were going somewhere together why didn't they go in the same car?"

"Oh, Sam," Penny said. "They didn't want anyone to know they were going anywhere together. That's just elementary."

We all agreed and then we were silent. I think we all must have been thinking the same thing. Why? Why didn't they want us to know they were going somewhere together? Strangely enough, nobody asked the question out loud. Not until Mary El, Janet, and I sat in my driveway.

"Why didn't they want anyone to know?" Janet asked.

We just looked at each other.

"Well, if you two won't say it, I will," Mary El said. "They've got two girls stashed away somewhere and they don't want us to know."

"That doesn't explain why they had to go in separate cars."

"Of course it does," said Mary El. "They wanted to throw us off the track. Phil doesn't want you to know, Cam, because he likes you . . . and Jeff is your good friend and he doesn't want to be in a position where you'll be asking him about Phil."

"This is true," Janet said.

"You think so?" I asked.

"I'm absolutely sure," Janet said. "I have vibes about it. Now we know these girls are whores or something, so they're no threat to you; we should all just forget about it."

I agreed and said good night. But alone in my room I couldn't forget about it. Maybe it was because I didn't really believe the "whore" theory . . . maybe because I didn't want to. Whatever the reason, I wasn't satisfied. Something wasn't ringing true. Yet I still couldn't find the truth or even touch on it . . . perhaps because I was afraid of the truth. I realize now that truth is never anything to be afraid of. Lies and deceit—particularly self-deceit—are the things we should fear most. But, then, anything was more acceptable than not knowing and by the time I fell asleep I had talked myself into believing what was the *least* uncomfortable. In other words, against all my principles, I'd bought the old sexist cliché that "boys will be boys." I couldn't help it; I'd sold out on every level. What a bummer!

Chapter 14

~~~~~~~~~~~~~~~~~~~~~~~~~~~~~~~~

Tuesdays I worked at the fabulous A&P from one to six so I had planned to clean my room and do horrible little chores in the morning. Then Mother reminded me that I had a dentist's appointment at eleven thirty. Normally, Mother would have gone off to New York before I woke up but because of the holiday the next day she'd canceled her New York appointments for the week and was having a mini-vacation. Naturally, since I had this appointment with the dentist, there was nothing else I could do that morning. I know that may sound strange but that's just the way I am. If I have one thing scheduled during the day at a particular time, I just can't start any other project. So I lay in bed reading magazines until ten thirty. Then I got up and showered (much to Rachel's disgust) and had a cup of coffee with Mother.

"Did you invite Phil?" she asked.

"Yes. He's coming. I didn't know what time to tell him though."

"Oh, I thought we'd eat about seven thirty . . . tell him to come around six."

"Is Rachel having one of her dippy friends?"

Mother smiled. "No. She won't be here. Donna is having a party and Rachel is going there."

I was thrilled. Just the four of us. It made me feel terribly grown up—just as though Mother and I were double-dating.

"Do you have a rehearsal tonight?"

"No. They're not rehearsing my scenes, so I have two days off. Why?"

"I thought maybe you could help me make the potato salad and cole slaw."

I nodded enthusiastically. Mother always made her own salads and I was surprised that she wanted help. I mean, how much was she going to make for four people?

Mother dropped me off at the dentist at eleven twenty-five. I walked in and sat on the couch while Dr. Dolan performed the finishing touches of torture on a very fat man who was breathtakingly ugly. Even though I knew this particular appointment was just a six-month checkup—a matter of poking around and some X rays—I couldn't help feeling sick to my stomach. Not exactly sick, I guess . . . more like a football team doing exercises inside me. The fat man left and Dr. Dolan motioned me in.

"And how have you been, Camilla?" she asked.

"Fine, until now," I said.

She laughed and rolled her eyes upward. "Oh, come on, you know I never hurt you."

I made some kind of grunt and sat in the chair. I knew nothing of the kind. Dr. Dolan had hurt me many a time. And I'll tell you something right here. Women dentists are not necessarily any more gentle than men dentists. My mother insists on using women whenever possible. She has a woman lawyer, a woman accountant, a woman doctor, and, of course, Dr. Dolan. Women dentists are the rarest of all. Frankly, I wish they were extinct. When we first moved up here I had a man dentist and I liked him very much. He hardly ever hurt me. Then Dr. Dolan opened her office and Mother switched. The only thing nice about having a woman dentist was that when you put your head back, sometimes the side of your head would press into her breasts and that was very comforting.

She tied the bib around me and I put my head back and looked up into her face. It was a very nice face ... very kindly and warm. Ha!

"Open," she said.

The torture would begin! Often, when I sat in the dentist's chair, I wondered why no one had ever used dentistry as a torture technique in wartime. I mean, just think of it. Suppose a person was captured by the enemy and they wanted to find out secrets. What is the one thing that practically everybody hates and fears? The Dentist! So why not take the prisoner and put him in the dentist chair and ask for the information while holding a buzzing drill above his mouth? Can you imagine? Okay ... so he still won't talk. So you pry his mouth open and you just start drilling, anywhere. ... Right through the center of a front tooth, for instance. It's too horrible to dwell on. I doubt whether anyone could withstand that kind of torture for very long. I think torturers have missed the boat by not using a truly universal horror: drilling teeth without anesthetic! Yuch!

"You have quite a bit of tartar, Camilla. I'll have to do some scraping."

"Today?" I asked, dreading the answer.

"Today."

So I had the scraping torture and then the X rays, which always made me gag a little, and it was over. Until the following Tuesday.

After dinner, when Mother dumped the potatoes on the table, I looked at her like she was nuts. There were pounds and pounds and pounds.

"What's that look?" she asked.

"That's a lot of potatoes. Do you think four people can really eat all that potato salad?"

"Four people? Oh, darling," she said, "there'll be twelve of us. I'm sorry, I thought I told you who was coming."

And then she told me. Besides us, there would be

four other couples. I couldn't help being a little disappointed but, still, it was a grown-up party and Mother had included me. I guess that was very nice of her. She could have asked me to find something else to do—I mean, she didn't have to invite me, did she? We started peeling.

I wanted very much to tell Mother what was going on with Jeff but I just didn't know how to begin. Then she gave me the opening.

"I hope you don't mind that I didn't tell you to invite Jeff and someone but I thought if you did that—well, your other friends might be hurt and I just couldn't have them all."

"I understand," I said. "I don't think Jeff would have come anyway. Something weird is going on." Then I told her everything, right through the night before. "What is it? What do you think?"

"I don't know what to think," she said.

That was very unlike Mother. She always had an opinion about everything.

"How much do you know about Phil?" she asked, going back to her peeling.

"Not much. I mean, what's to know?"

She shrugged.

"Do you think they have some girls somewhere?"

"It's possible."

"But you don't think so, do you?"

"Honey, I honestly have no way of knowing what's going on. I don't even know one of the boys."

"But you must have some ideas . . . some speculation."

"Speculation can be very destructive. Eventually, I'm sure you'll find out what it is and when you do, it'll probably be some silly thing that everyone will laugh about."

I was disappointed that Mother wasn't going to be any help.

"Are you angry with me?" she asked, beginning to slice the potatoes.

"No."

"But you *are* disappointed that I don't have a neat little answer for you."

"I guess."

"Camilla," she said, "I'm not brushing you off. All I'm saying is this: If what's going on with Jeff and Phil is important, there will be plenty of time to react when you find out what it is."

"I know . . . don't project."

"Exactly," she said, giving me a big smile.

After that we rapped about different things but I felt a kind of distance between us. In fact, I was very much alone that night. I felt far away from Mother, Jeff and I were almost like strangers, and Phil seemed more remote than he ever had.

We finished the potato salad about nine and Mother said she wanted to do the cole slaw alone. That made me feel even worse. Not that I love making cole slaw but I thought she just wanted to get rid of me. On the other hand, maybe she wanted to be alone so she could think about Ray. I certainly understood that need. That's exactly what I wanted to do—think about Phil. So I said good night and went up to my room. Once I got there I found that it wasn't so easy to think about him, at least not in a pure way. By that I mean thinking of Phil alone. I don't know exactly what it is you think when you think of a person you're hung up on. . . . I guess you think of the way he looks and you think his name and you think of things that have happened between you and how he said this or that and how he looked at you. But when I tried, it didn't work too well. Always, when I closed my eyes and tried to picture him, I would see Jeff's face as well, and if I just thought his name it came out: Phil and Jeff. For the first time in all the years I had known and loved Jeff, I hated him. I couldn't believe I was feeling that and yet there was no denying it. I hated Jeff! And I wasn't even sure why. Well, to hell with him. Tomorrow night I would have Phil all to myself and surely everything would be straightened out. . . . I thought.

Janet, Mary El, and Sam came over about eleven and we spent the day on our beach. Sam had made ham-and-cheese sandwiches on rye and I supplied the Cokes. It was a beautiful, hot day and I felt particularly sorry for Janet, sitting on the beach in her green slacks and plaid sleeveless shirt. She wouldn't wear a bathing suit because of her weight. She even went in swimming in her clothes. We tried to convince her at least to take her slacks off . . . after all, it was only us . . . but no amount of pleading did any good. Mary El was in heaven because she got to spend the day with Sam, and even Sam was in a fairly good mood because Linda was out of town and he didn't have to be plotting how he might see her.

By mutual but silent consent, no one mentioned Jeff of Phil until sometime in the afternoon.

"Are you coming to the party tonight with Phil?" Sam asked.

"No. My mother's having a barbecue and Phil is coming here."

"You're going to miss Eben's party?" Mary El said. "It's going to be a neat party. He's getting a keg of beer . . . or at least that's what he says."

"You mean, his mother is going to let him do that?"

"His mother's away."

Eben's father was dead. He had died two years before of a heart attack and Eben had never quite gotten over it. He was the youngest of three children; the other two were married and lived far away, and Eben felt he had to take care of his mother. His father had been in real estate and they'd had lots of money, but he'd never saved any and so, when his father died, they had just enough to buy a small house in Southold. His mother worked in a real estate agency and Eben worked every minute he wasn't in school to help make ends meet. It was also rumored that he sold pot but no one was sure of that. None of us had ever seen him smoke any, nor, for that matter, had he ever tried to sell it to any of us. Not that he would have had many takers. I had tried pot once, but since I wasn't a smoker, it just made me cough a lot and I hated the smell and taste.

Drugs were something I was definitely not interested in. Nor were any of my friends. I suppose a lot of kids would think we were square . . . but, well, mostly we got high on ourselves and the things we did and an occasional sip of Boone's Farm wine. But even that wasn't excessive. I don't mean to sound like a Pollyanna . . . and it wasn't for moral reasons that we didn't blow dope or drink hard stuff—it was just that no one felt a real need to. Except maybe for Penny, who had a thing for tequila. And then, of course, there was Maura, who'd been known to put it away. But so far this year she didn't seem to be doing any drinking . . . at least not around the theater. Of course, we didn't have any way of knowing what she did with her private life because she still never really spent any time with us.

The night of the horrible incident with the black kids was the only time she ever joined us after rehearsal. I guess it wasn't her fault though. Her parents were very strict and wanted her home early. At least that's what she said, Maura! Suddenly it struck me. Why hadn't I thought of it before? Why had I forgotten?

"Maura," I said, out loud.

They all looked at me.

"I beg your pardon?" said Mary El.

"Maura."

"I thought that's what you said." She turned to Janet. "Is she having some sort of attack, or what?"

"How could I be so dumb?"

"I never thought you'd ask," Mary El said.

"Shut up," Sam said. "What's wrong, Camilla?"

"I'll bet anything it's Maura Harris."

"What is, for God's sake?" Mary El said, exasperated.

"Jeff?" Janet was so wise.

"Yes. Remember how he defended her in the beginning? I thought then that he had a thing for her. He denied it, of course. But I'll bet anything that that's what Jeff's been doing."

"So why would it have to be a secret?" Sam asked.

"And what's it got to do with Phil?"

"I thought you might ask that! You know that girl who plays the piano—Connie what's-her-name? Well, someone told me a few days ago that she has a terrible crush on Phil."

"So?"

"So who drives home every night with Maura?"

"Connie what's-her-name," the three of them said together.

"Exactly."

"You mean," Mary El said, finally getting into the swing of it, "Phil and Jeff are meeting Connie and Maura?"

"Yes."

"Gross!"

"He sure did come to her aid the night of the ambush," Sam said.

"But if that's true, why would Phil be coming to your barbecue tonight?"

"Well, I think he likes me."

"And what about Connie?" Janet asked. "Why isn't he seeing her tonight? Why isn't he taking her to Eben's party—or at least meeting her there?"

"I don't know, except maybe—well, maybe Maura and Connie . . . you know?"

They all looked at me blankly.

"What I mean is . . . maybe Jeff and Phil are messing around with them late at night and that's all they want from them."

"Sometimes you're archaic, Camilla," Sam said. "What are you saying? Maura and Connie are *bad* girls and you're good and all that jazz?"

"Of course not." But I was. And I guess I *was* archaic. Maybe I had read too much Jane Austen! "I don't know what I'm saying. I mean, maybe I don't have all the reasons right but I bet that I'm right about Jeff and Phil seeing them."

Janet agreed that I might be onto something and they all decided to keep a close watch on Jeff and Maura at the party. At least, we decided, it was the first idea we'd had about Jeff and Phil that made sense. Then Janet decided that sometime during my evening I should swing the conversation around to Maura and Connie and see how Phil reacted. We'd all confer, somehow, around midnight.

Ray had arrived on the three o'clock boat and he was just as neat as I'd remembered. Mother gave him the small guest room down the hall from me. Now, I thought it was really silly to make him sleep in the guest room—I mean, I wasn't a child in these matters and I told Mother that when we were alone for a minute.

"There's no need to put Ray in the guest room," I said.

Mother looked at me, her head cocked to one side. "What does that mean?"

"It means, I'm not a child."

"I'm not following you, Camilla."

"Look," I said, "I'm sixteen years old."

"I'm well aware of how old you are, darling."

"What I'm trying to say is that it's perfectly all right with me if you and Ray share the same room."

"Well," she said, trying not to smile, and crossing her arms in front of her, "it doesn't happen to be perfectly all right with me."

"But I don't care," I said.

"But I *do*."

"You're being archaic," I said.

"Camilla, do you think it's too much to ask that you allow me to conduct my life the way I see fit?"

"Well, don't tell me you haven't slept with him."

"All right, I won't tell you."

"Haven't you?" I asked, appalled.

"Darling . . . I know you and I have been very open

about things but, frankly, I don't want to discuss my sex life with you. I think it's terrific that you're so free and liberated, but try to remember ... I'm a fugitive from the fifties and you'll have to give me time to catch up with you. Okay?"

I shrugged. "I just wanted you to know that I'm open," I said.

"Thank you, dear. I appreciate that."

She kissed me lightly on the forehead and went off to the kitchen. I wondered if she knew how lucky she was to have me for a daughter. I also wondered why they called it the Fabulous Fifties.

Even though it was a pretty hot day, Ray and I decided we'd shoot some baskets. I happen to be very good at basketball and I dearly love it. Ray wasn't bad for someone his age. We played two out of three games of O-U-T and I won. Even though I'm not terribly tall I have very strong arms and I'm able to make long shots. That's how I beat him. He was good at lay-ups but I'm good at both. After the game we went for a swim and then we sat on the beach for a little while. I thought about telling him that it was all right with me if he shared a room with Mother but decided against it when I realized Mother might think that was interference.

We made some small talk and then he said to me, "Laura tells me you want to be an actress."

"Yes. I don't know if I'm any good or not though."

"Don't you?" he asked, smiling at me.

I smiled back. "Well, yes, I guess I do. I mean, well, I'm not bad."

"I'll bet you're damn good," he said. "I hope I'll be able to see your show."

"That'd be great."

"I have a brother in show business. Did you ever hear of Jack Fowler?"

I had indeed. He was a well-known director and just that past year had done a revival of a Hellman play that had gotten raves. "Sure. He's your brother?"

He nodded. "Maybe when the time comes Jack could help you."

"Oh, neat." I wanted to ask him if he could get his brother to come up to see *Anything Goes* but decided that that was just too pushy.

While I took my shower I thought about the conversation I'd had with Phil that morning on the phone. I called to tell him what time to come and he seemed glad to hear from me. He told me a little bit about the previous night's rehearsal and a story about Bruce and Debbie who were caught by Stimpson in the graveyard behind the theater. They had been sitting on a baby's grave, making out, when she'd found them. All in all, it was a good conversation and I looked forward to the evening. Most of all I was pleased because Phil hadn't mentioned Jeff once.

Chapter 15

People started arriving at six. The Rosenbergs were the first. I like them . . . and I think part of the reason I do is because they like each other so much. It's not often you get to meet a married couple that really like each other. Ben and Ruth Rosenberg are devoted to each other and although they don't have any children, they write children's books, together.

Another reason I like them is because they're tiny. There is something dear and cuddly about both of them. But most of all I like them because they never treat me like a child, the way most of Mother's other friends do. Ruth always asks me my opinions and I know she takes my answers seriously. And Ben does the same thing. I am a person to them and that makes me feel good. I was very glad they were the first to arrive.

After I got them their drinks they started a conversation about Watergate which, I have to confess, I really knew very little about.

"There is no doubt in my mind," Ruth said, "that Haldeman is lying."

Ben nodded in agreement.

"What do you think, Camilla?" Ruth asked.

"Well," I said, desperately trying to remember which one Haldeman was, "I think . . . the truth is I just don't know enough about it to answer that."

There was a moment of silence and then Ruth slapped her tiny knee with her tiny hand. "Good for you," she said. "I like a person who admits she doesn't know something. That's an admirable quality. But you should read up on it, Cam. History's in the making."

I said I would and then other people started arriving The Corwins: She's tall and thin and constantly blinks her eyes and giggles, and he's quiet and shorter than she and smokes a pipe. The Tuckers: They own the local newspaper and have twelve children and four marriages between them. He looks a little bit like Nixon except he's younger and better-looking and laughs a lot and she's very glamorous and terribly funny and tells lots of interesting stories. They often dance in the aisles of the A&P to the piped-in music because they say there's nowhere to dance out here. I like them too. The last of Mother's friends to arrive were the Braunschweigs. She's a painter and sells her oils in a little shop in Southold, and he's a framer. They're both very tall and very attractive. She, Yolanda, is Italian and usually smiling and she expresses herself very eloquently. He, Jim, is German and seldom smiles and when you talk to him he mostly says: "Yeah, what the hell, listen." Which almost always comes out sounding: "Yeahwhatthehelllissen." They all knew each other, except for Ray of course, so there was no problem with conversation.

It was twenty of seven when Phil arrived.

"I'm sorry I'm late," he said.

"That's all right."

"No, it's not. I like to be punctual. I'm really sorry."

"It's okay. Would you like something to drink before we go out on the porch and meet everyone?"

I took Phil out to the kitchen and got him a Coke. He was very silent and I just couldn't think of a thing to say. I guess you could say it was a tense situation. Then Mother came into the kitchen and I introduced them.

I could tell Mother was looking him over very carefully. But only *I* could tell. It wasn't the kind of once-over that some mothers gave, making the boy or girl feel like a victim or something. It was quite subtle. I guess Mother had developed it over the years while observing patients. Anyway, only someone who knew her very well, like me, would know what she was doing.

"We're very glad you could come, Phil."

"Thank you," he said. "I'm glad you invited me."

Mother smiled and said that he should come out to the porch and meet everyone.

When she introduced him, everyone treated him like a regular guest except Mrs. Corwin. She had to blow it by saying:

"Oh, Cammy, is this your little boyfriend?"

I honestly didn't know what to say to that but Ruth Rosenberg quickly stepped in and asked Phil if he was in the show with me, which got everyone discussing Youth On Stage and its merits. Everything went quite well from there on and I was really proud of Phil, who handled himself terrifically.

Mother and I did the chicken barbecue and Ray got Phil to help him with drinks. Dinner was served buffet style and Phil and I sat in the living room to eat. Jim Braunschweig and Ray joined us.

We talked about living in the country and whether young people should try city living before settling down in places like Southold.

"Are you going to try a city after college, Phil?" Ray asked.

"I don't know. I'm not sure I'm the city type."

"Yeahwhatthehelllissen."

"I guess I'll have to if I want to act," I said.

"Well, you're definitely a city type," Phil said.

"How do you know?"

"I can just tell."

"I agree with Phil," Ray said.

"Yeahwhatthehelllissen."

During dessert Mother joined us.

"I understand you're a fan of Judy Garland's," Phil said to Mother.

"Yes, I am."

"So is Phil," I said.

Phil said, "I have all of her records."

"Yeahwhatthehelllissen."

"My mother's a fan, too—that's how I know about her. My father hates her. He says she was a drunk and a pillhead and . . . well, he just hates her. I don't know what it is about her—something just gets to me."

"I saw her play the Palace," Mother said. "It was quite an experience."

"I never saw her in person. It's one of the regrets of my life," Phil said.

"Yeahwhatthehelllissen."

When dessert was over, Mother, Ray, and Jim went back out to the porch and Phil and I were alone. He hadn't really paid much attention to me. Not that he'd been rude or anything but he just hadn't paid any special attention.

"Is something wrong tonight, Phil?" I asked.

"Wrong? No . . . I don't think so. Why?"

"I don't know—you seem kind of far away."

"I'm sorry," he said. "I was wondering, Camilla, do you think your mother would mind . . . I mean, well, do you think it would be all right if we left in a little while?"

I don't think there had ever been a moment like that in my life before. Phil wanted to be alone with me! Oh, there were plenty of times when Harlan had wanted to be alone with me but I had never wanted to be alone with him. This was an entirely different matter. We *both* wanted to be alone! I was really flipped out that Phil felt that way. He'd been acting so strange, so distant, that I thought he'd lost interest. For the first time in days I didn't give a damn what he and Jeff were doing or who they were seeing. What did it matter? In the grander scheme of things, Phil wanted to be with me!

"I'm sure she wouldn't mind," I said. "I'll go tell her."

Of course, she didn't mind. She asked where we

were going and I said for a ride and she said not to come home too late because I had to work the next day. We said good night to everyone and were off.

As I clicked my seat belt into place I couldn't remember ever being so happy. I had no idea that this would turn out to be the most horrible night of any life, to date.

We were silent as we drove down Bayview Avenue but I was feeling so good that I didn't find the silence awkward. I noticed that Phil was speeding, which was unusual for him, but I didn't make anything of it then. I wondered if he would take me to Kenny's Beach or if we would just drive around. Before I knew it we were going through the center of Southold and then he made a right turn at Locust Lane.

"Where are we going?" I asked.

"To the party," he said, sounding surprised that I was asking.

The party! It had never occurred to me. What a jerk I'd been. No wonder he was driving so fast! He didn't want to be alone with me at all. Far from it. What he wanted was to be with tons of other kids— and maybe to be with one, but that one wasn't me. It was probably Connie what's-her-name. I couldn't think of anything to say and now the silence became deadly. At least for me. As we neared Eben's house I could hear the noise and music.

The party was taking place mostly in the backyard. We walked around the side of the house. It seemed like hundreds of kids were there. And there *was* a keg of beer. It was the only thing Eben came through on all summer. Kids said hello to us and I tried to look happy. I looked for Mary El and Janet but they didn't seem to be there. Maura Harris and Connie were there though and, sure enough, Jeff was sitting with them under a tree.

"There's Jeff. Come on," Phil said and headed for the trio. I had no intention of being a fifth wheel so I let him go ahead of me. He didn't even notice that I wasn't with him. Phil sat down on the ground and soon all four were laughing together. I think I was mostly shocked that he could be so callous. I mean, didn't it occur to him that I might be hurt? That I might care that he was so interested in Connie? I'd had no idea he could be so cruel. But I guess maybe when you're in love you lose your perspective. Obviously, I had. Quickly I looked around for someone to talk to. I wasn't about to stand there like some unwanted idiot.

A lot of the kids were sitting in a big circle on the ground playing a game. I walked over and pretended I was interested in finding out what the game was. Eben seemed to be running it and from what I could understand it was some word thing that involved everyone being some kind of shit—like Cat, Rat, Dog, Tree, or whatever. I spotted Tina sitting on a chaise by herself and I joined her.

"How come you're sitting here by yourself?"

"I think it's a vulgar game. Sometimes I wonder about Eben."

"Yeah, I know what you mean."

Tina and I never had too much to say to each other so we just sort of sat and watched everyone. Then I spotted Mary El and Janet coming into the yard from the house. I waved to them and they came over.

"What are you doing here?" Janet asked.

I indicated, without looking at it, the spot where Phil and the trio sat.

Janet, Mary El, and Tina looked in that direction, then back to me. Their faces were blank.

"I don't get it," Mary El said.

"Are you blind?" I said.

"Must be."

I turned. Maura and Connie were sitting with Maura's brother Jim and two other boys. Phil and Jeff were gone.

"I . . . well, Phil wanted to come to the party. He

went directly over to Maura, Connie, and Jeff when we came in."

"Yeah, well, they ain't there now, kid," Mary El said. I nodded.

"You want me to ask Maura where they went?" Janet asked.

I didn't. We decided to go out front and see if their cars were still there. They were. We came back to the party, looked in the house and all around the yard. Jeff and Phil were nowhere to be seen.

The game broke up and everybody started dancing. Janet, Mary El, Sam, and I stood near the house and scanned the yard. Suddenly, Sam said, "Look!" He pointed to a clump of trees at the end of the yard. Phil came reeling out and hit the ground. Bruce flew out after him and jumped on top of him. Then Jeff and Harlan rolled out from the trees, their fists flying. Quickly, everyone stopped dancing and ran toward the fight.

"Come on," Janet said, and dragged me down the yard.

It was horrible. It had been a long time since I'd seen boys fighting, and the sound of hard fists hitting flesh was awful. Everyone started screaming and then Eben, Sam, Walt, and Jim stepped in and tried to pull them apart. It seemed like hours before the fight stopped but finally it was over. Eben had Jeff around the waist, Sam had Phil, Walt held back Bruce, and Jim was struggling with Harlan. They were all huffing and puffing. Jeff's nose was bleeding and Phil had a cut on his cheek. The other two were bleeding also.

"What's goin' on?" Eben said, between gasps for air.

"Faggots," Bruce said, "these guys are faggots."

"Huh?"

"They're queers, man," Harlan sputtered.

Eben let go of Jeff as though he'd been burned.

"We went in the bushes to . . . you know," Bruce said, suddenly becoming shy in front of all the girls, "and we found these two creeps kissing, for godsake."

"They're goddamn queers," Harlan said.

Faggots . . . queers . . . fairies . . . the murmur echoed over the yard. Phil and Jeff said nothing and looked at no one.

"You gotta be kiddin'," Eben said.

"Ask them—ask the fags."

Sam slowly let go of Phil, and softly he said, "Is it true?"

Phil turned and looked at Sam. Everything was quiet and even the music had stopped. My head was spinning as bits and pieces of the last few days whirled in my mind.

"Jeff?" Sam asked, softly.

Jeff took out a handkerchief and wiped at the blood on his face. He smeared it, which made him look even more wounded than he was.

"C'mon, creep, answer," Eben barked.

"Shut up," Sam said. "Jeff, tell these guys they're full of it."

"I told you," Harlan yelled, "they're flaming fags!"

Jeff looked so pathetic standing there, blood all over his face, his head down, blond hair clotted with dirt, that all my old feelings about him came back to me. I pushed past Penny and Tina who were standing in front of me and ran to him. I took his hand.

"Tell them, Jeff . . . tell them it isn't true."

He looked at me a long moment and then I saw the tears running down his face making streaks in the blood.

"Phil," I yelled, "say something."

"What do you want me to say, Camilla?"

"Tell these people that Bruce and Harlan are lying."

Phil looked at Jeff, who looked back at him.

"Buzz off, Camilla, we're not lying. We saw them," Bruce yelled.

Suddenly, I found myself saying something I had no intention of saying. "Well, I happen to be in a position to know it couldn't be true."

"Don't, Camilla," Phil said, softly.

"You saying you made it with Chrystie or something?" asked Harlan. "Huh?"

"So what? That doesn't mean a thing," someone else said. "So he's ac-dc—he's still a fag in my book."

I felt crazy. Jeff and Phil just stood there saying nothing, listening to all the accusations and saying nothing. Why didn't they defend themselves?

Then someone started screaming. "Tell them . . . tell them it isn't true . . . tell them. . . ." The voice was loud, shrill, piercing and I couldn't place it. And then I felt Janet's arm around me.

"Don't, Camel, don't," she whispered.

And I knew then the screaming voice was me.

"Take it easy, kid," Penny said.

"Oh, please," I cried, "please say *something.*"

Jeff tossed his hair back from his eyes, looked directly into mine and spoke the words I won't ever forget if I live to be one hundred and ninety.

"Okay . . . okay, if you want to hear it so much: It's true. Phil and I love each other."

Behind me, I heard some giggles and some murmuring and a lot of movement. But I could say nothing and I definitely couldn't move.

"Get the hell off my property," I heard Eben say. "We don't want fags around here."

I watched, immobile, as Jeff and Phil started walking toward the crowd that ringed them. They stopped for a moment and waited until the kids parted to let them pass. Harlan stepped forward and blocked their way.

"You guys make me want to puke," he said.

Jeff put his arm lightly across Phil's shoulder and said, "Let us by, Young, we're not hurting you."

"Make me," Harlan said.

Sam stepped over to Harlan and pulled him out of the way. "Cool it, Harlan. Let them go."

"Yeah, let 'em go . . . we don't want 'em."

"Ain't they cute."

"Thay, thweetie!"

There were whistles and jeers and hoots and more remarks as Jeff and Phil kept walking. The kids followed them and somebody threw dirt and somebody else threw a soda can and Jim Harris stuck out his foot and Jeff tripped and fell to the ground. The shouts and jeers got louder as Phil bent down to help Jeff up. And finally they rounded the corner of the house and were out of sight. Some of the kids followed them to their cars, I guess, because we could still hear shouts for a few minutes. Then I heard two cars start up and take off down the street.

"Goddamn faries," Eben said.

And before I knew what was happing I was pounding Eben's chest and scratching at his face and screaming.

The next thing I knew I was sitting in Mary El's car between Mary El and Janet. Sam, Penny, and Walt were in the back seat.

"You want to go home or what?" Janet asked.

I shook my head. "Not yet."

She nodded and signaled to Mary El, who started the car. I don't know where we drove that night, I just know we drove around for a long time saying nothing. Occasionally, somebody would ask for a cigarette or ask to have the window opened or closed but that was about all.

Finally, Mary El said she was getting low on gas and everybody agreed we should go home. Janet asked me if I wanted to stay overnight at her house but I didn't. They dropped me off about one and we arranged to meet for lunch at the Sweet Shop at twelve thirty. I supposed we would discuss it all then.

The lights were out, except for one in the living room. I knew I should go to bed because I had to get up early for work but I couldn't bring myself to go up right away. Instead, I went into the living room and turned on Mother's stereo. I plugged in the earphones and started looking through the records. Finally, I found what I was looking for.

I put on the earphones and sat on the couch. There were two records in the album and I'd put them on at random. The first song was "Come Rain or Come Shine," Judy Garland at Carnegie Hall.

I'd heard the songs before when Mother played them, but I'd never paid too much attention. Now Garland's voice seemed to be cutting me in two. When she started singing "The Man That Got Away," I started crying silently. Somehow, I couldn't cry out loud. I've noticed that I never can when I'm alone. The tears ran down my face as her voice rang in my ears. My eyes were closed. Then something made me open them.

Ray was standing a few feet away from me. He said something but I couldn't hear him so I took off the earphones.

"I said, you gave me one helluva fright," he said. "You look like something from outer space with those things on."

I forced a smile. He came closer, taking a pack of cigarettes from his robe pocket. "I came down for a glass of milk."

I couldn't say anything.

"You want a glass of milk?" he asked.

I shook my head.

He offered me a cigarette and I shook my head again.

"You want me to go away?"

I shrugged.

"Can you talk about it? Would you like me to call Laura?"

I finally found my voice. "No. No to both."

"Okay." He sat down next to me on the couch.

I wanted desperately to tell him everything but I couldn't. I had to think about it all first. If I told him he'd tell Mother and I didn't want to discuss it with her yet. It seemed I couldn't do anything but cry. The tears started again and this time some sound came with them. Gently, Ray put his arm around me and I put my head on his shoulder. He stroked my hair as I cried.

Much later, he led me upstairs to my room, helped me off with my shoes, and threw a sheet over me. There was no way I could have gotten undressed and Ray knew that. He kissed me on the cheek and turned out the light. Exhausted, I feel asleep immediately.

Chapter 16

I awoke very early and decided to take a walk on the beach before breakfast. There was so much to think about. First of all, there was Jeff. Phil was another matter; I'd really only known him a short time. But Jeff! I'd known him for years. How could it be true? Jeff liked girls . . . didn't he? There had been Tina last summer, and—and what? It really hadn't worked out with her, had it? And Jeff never really dated. Lots of girls were interested in him but it was a one-way street. He never said he didn't like girls so I just assumed he did. I guess a lot of what we think about people is what we assume, or what we want to believe. When there are gaps, we just fill them in with the colors we like best. But how could Jeff be a *queer*? I mean, queers were . . . were what? I realized I didn't really know. All I knew was that some of the guys made jokes, lisping and bending their wrists, and when I'd lived in the Village I'd seen guys in makeup and women's clothes. And, of course, there had been Paul Shultz.

Paul was a senior when I was a freshman so I really didn't know him, but I knew of him. Everyone did. He was tall and thin and wore his long red hair in a fluffy ponytail with a big green ribbon. He also wore eye makeup. Everyone made fun of him and called him names but Paul never seemed to care. He'd just wiggle his hips and squeal things like, "Don't knock it 'til you've tried it, sweetheart!"

But Phil and Jeff were nothing like that. My knowledge of homosexuals was very limited. Still, I couldn't believe that Jeff was really a homosexual. Why hadn't he told me? We told each other everything. Didn't he know I would have tried to understand . . . to help him?

And Phil. My Phil. I heard Jeff's words again: "Phil and I love each other." My best friend and my boyfriend loved each other! How could it be possible? My best friend had *stolen* my boyfriend. It seemed so crazy. I had been really convinced that Phil cared for me. He certainly was the first boy that I had really cared for . . . loved. Sure, I had had lots of crushes, but Phil was different. I had to laugh. He sure was different!

Even while I was thinking all this stuff I wasn't really feeling anything. I guess it was because I couldn't actually believe it. It was as though I was thinking about two people I didn't really know—two people I had seen in a movie or read about. I couldn't connect what was in my head with my viscera. I wondered when it would hit me.

When I got back to the house everybody was still asleep. I was very glad because the last thing I wanted to do was talk. I had a quick glass of orange juice and a small bowl of granola, and before I went out to the road to wait for Mrs. Ahlers and Sam, I went into Mother's office and got out the big Random House dictionary. I looked up homosexuality. This is what it said: *Sexual desire or behavior directed toward a person or persons of one's own sex.* Thanks a lot!

Mary El and Janet were waiting for Sam and me when we came out of the A&P at twelve thirty.

"We brought you sandwiches," Mary El said. "The Sweet Shop is too crowded, as usual."

We drove up to Rocky Point in East Marion and parked. I opened up my sandwich. Peanut butter, jelly, and marshmallow. I took a bite and felt everything stick to the roof of my mouth. I wasn't sure I would be able to eat.

"Well," Janet said, "what are we going to do?"

"Do?" Sam asked.

"Do," Janet repeated. She took out a pack of Trues and lit one.

"What are you doing?" I asked. Janet never smoked. In fact, she thought smoking was a disgusting habit.

"I'm smoking."

"I can see that. How come?"

"It's her second pack since last night," Mary El said. "Gross."

"I can't help myself," Janet said quickly. "I have to do something. So, what do you think?"

"About your smoking?" Sam asked.

She groaned. "About Phil and Jeff, of course."

"Oh, that. What's to think?"

"Well, don't you care? Surely *you* care, Camilla."

"Don't you think it's gross?" Mary El asked.

"Have either of you thought what it means?" Janet said.

"Means?"

Mary El and Janet looked at each other and rolled their eyes. "Camilla," Janet said, "Phil and Jeff are part of our crowd. What will people think?"

"And Phil is your boyfriend . . . and Jeff's a close friend of yours," Mary El added.

"People will think we're all a bunch of queers," said Janet.

"I find that hard to believe," I said.

"She's just not thinking," Mary El said to Janet.

"This we know. The point is they can't hang around with us anymore."

"What makes you think they'll want to?" Sam asked. "They'll probably just want to be with each other. Isn't that what happens when you fall in love?"

"Oh, don't even say that, Sam . . . it's too gross." Mary El shook herself.

"Well, that's how my Linda and that Burt are; they always want to be alone together."

"Oh, Sam," Janet said, "that is normal. You can't compare Linda and Burt's love with Phil's and Jeff's."

Sam slid down in his seat. "What's normal about a beautiful woman like Linda loving a jerk like Burt?"

"We are not getting into the Linda–Burt thing now," Janet said. "Phil and Jeff are our problem."

"Why?" I asked.

"Why what?"

"Why are they our problem?"

"Honestly, Camilla, are you being purposely vague? First of all," Janet said, "they are involved in the show with us—we'll be seeing them every night. We have to have some sort of standard . . . some point of view."

"Maybe they'll quit the show," Sam said.

"Never," said Janet.

"Look," I said, "if Phil and Jeff . . . if Phil and Jeff are . . ." I couldn't bring myself to say the words. I was beginning to feel something. Disgust? I wasn't sure. But something.

"We have to freeze them out," Mary El said.

"They're undesirables," Janet said. "We'll give them the silent treatment. That way they'll know what we think of them and so will the other kids. I mean, we don't want to be associated with them, do we?"

"Jeff drives me to the theater every night," I said.

"I'll pick you up," Mary El said.

I found myself agreeing with them although I wasn't really sure why. I couldn't imagine what it would be like never talking to Jeff but, on the other hand, I couldn't conceive of what I could possibly say to him now.

The afternoon went even slower than usual. On my break, Maura sat down on a wooden case next to me. We were in the stockroom.

"Hi, guy," she said. "Have you seen the gold-dust twins since last night?"

At first I didn't know what she was talking about and then I realized she meant Phil and Jeff. I shook my head.

"I hear you're hung up on Phil."

"Oh, I dated him a few times, that's all."

"They must have been real far-out dates," she said, and giggled.

"I had a good time with him. He's a nice guy."

"Yeah, real sweet," she said. "Jeff's the one that gets me—I thought he was an okay guy. Who would of thunk it!"

"He is . . . an okay guy."

"Adorable," she said, and threw her paper cup in the basket. "Well, see you tonight in fairyland. Wow! What a bummer it's turning out to be."

After work I had Mrs. Ahlers drop me in Southold. I wanted to go to Elissa's Bookstore and see if there were any books on homosexuality.

Elissa's was one of the coziest and nicest bookstores I'd ever been in. And Elissa herself was one of the nicest people I'd ever met. Lots of the kids went to the shop just to hang out and talk to her. She was always ready to listen if you had a problem and to give you a cup of free coffee and a cookie. The store had been open for about two years. Elissa was from New York, originally the Bronx, but the local people had accepted her very quickly. Usually it took about thirty years before they stopped looking at you like you were from Mars or something. I guess they accepted her because she was always so warm and sunny and even when you were feeling lousy she made you kind of glow inside.

"Hi, Camilla," she said when I walked in. "I haven't seen you for a while—you haven't given up reading, have you?"

"No. I've just been awfully busy with the show."

"How's it going?"

"Pretty good. Are you going to come see it?"

"Are you kidding? An earthquake couldn't stop me."

And I knew that was true. Elissa always came to everything the kids did. For instance, this past June she came to an assembly to hear Billy Shipley give his campaign speech for president of student council.

Billy's parents weren't even there. That's just the kind of person she was.

"Want a cup of coffee? I'm out of cookies but coffee water's on. What's the matter? You look a little down in the dumps."

I thought about telling her but decided that the fewer people who knew about it, the better. She'd find out sooner or later, anyhow.

"I have my period," I said, which was true. Now I wasn't one of those girls who made a big deal out of getting my period but sometimes it did make me feel a little low.

"You have cramps?" she asked. "It's all in your mind, you know. I used to get terrible cramps but once I accepted that it was just something that was going to happen once a month for the next thousand years, well, the cramps went away."

"No, I don't get cramps."

"Good. You get depressed though, huh? Makes you feel a little meshugana? That means crazy," she said. "I always forget up here they don't know from meshugana."

"You always forget I lived in New York until a few years ago."

"Oh, that's right. That's why I like you—you're a real mensch." She laughed and her black curls shook around her face. "So, you want something special or did you just come in to schmooze?"

"I'll just look around a little."

"Sure—look . . . enjoy."

It would have been a lot simpler if I'd just asked Elissa if she had any good books on homosexuality but, frankly, I was too embarrassed. I mean, how would I explain it? Not that I'd have to . . . I mean, Elissa never made you feel foolish about the books you bought, but, well, what would she think? I suppose I could have said I was doing a paper on it or something—but I think she would have known that in Southold you just don't do papers on things like that. Besides, this was July!

I started looking through the paperbacks. Mysteries, novels, gothics, nonfiction, science fiction . . . and then I saw it: *Everything You Always Wanted To Know About Sex—But Were Afraid to Ask*. Well, that sure was me. I was definitely afraid to ask. I turned immediately to the index and looked under H. It was there all right. "Homosexuality, 159–187." Even though I knew Elissa wouldn't care, I felt creepy about buying that book, so I picked up a copy of *Jennie*, Vol. 1, to kind of balance it out. I brought them up to the desk.

"Oh, you'll enjoy that," she said, writing up *Jennie*. She said nothing about the other one.

As I was leaving she said: "Come back when you have more time and we can rap. Okay? Give my best to Laura and tell her it's been too long."

On Route 25 I stuck out my thumb and got a ride from a woman who lived down the road from us.

I put the books in my room but didn't have time to read anything because Mother said dinner was ready. She and Ray were going to the movies. I gathered Ray hadn't said anything to Mother about the night before because she casually asked me if I'd had a good time. I said I had and Ray and I exchanged a look while I gave Rachel a kick under the table. Ray's keeping our secret made me like him even more. Mother also said she thought Phil seemed like a perfectly nice boy which made me know that she really didn't think he was too special. Whenever Mother said anyone was perfectly nice it meant she thought they were actually a little dull. Normally, I would have pursued it, but under the circumstances, I didn't really want to talk about Phil.

Ray and Mother left at seven and I washed up the dishes and then went outside to wait for Mary El and Janet. I was standing on the road in front of our fence when Jeff pulled up. I had forgotten to tell him I wouldn't be going with him. I didn't know what to do. I stared at him and he stared back.

Finally he said, "Are you coming?"

"I'm waiting for Mary El," I said weakly.

He pulled away, his tires squealing. Then he slammed on his brakes and went into reverse. He came to a screeching halt next to me.

"You know what you are, Camilla?" he yelled, his face red. "You're a goddamn turncoat and you make me . . . Oh, to hell with it." And he pulled away again.

At first I was hurt and then I got mad. *I* was a turncoat! Well, what was he? He was a Benedict Arnold, that's what he was. What did he expect? He'd stolen my boyfriend, after all. I couldn't believe the words as I thought them. It just didn't make sense. Jeff, Jeff, Jeff, how could you do it? It would have been bad enough if he'd turned out to be queer with someone else . . . but Phil. For me it was a double whammy. I felt like I was going to cry and then I saw Mary El's car coming down the road so I swallowed my tears and tried to look bright and cheery.

Naturally, everyone connected with YOS knew about Phil and Jeff by the time rehearsal started. There were whispers and giggles and even some pointing . . . and plenty of jokes. During the "Take Me Back to Manhattan" dance Maura and Penny bumped into each other and started giggling.

MAURA: Oh, sweetie, I didn't know you cared.
PENNY: You just never noticed, darling.
MAURA: You want to get it on?
PENNY: Any time.

There were great guffaws from Bruce and Harlan and that bunch. Later, Eben pinched Walt's cheek and Walt did a pirouette and fell into Eben's arms.

WALT: Oh, you're tho thtwong.
EBEN: That's this week, honey. Next week it's your turn.

More giggles and laughter. After the third reference, which involved Bruce McDonald and Jim Harris, Stimpson blew her whistle.

"Listen, I don't know what's going on here tonight but we could do without the homosexual jokes. I don't like them any more than antiblack, anti-Jewish, or anti-anything else."

"How about Aunty Phil," a voice came from the chorus.

After the laughter died down, Stimpson went on.

"I'm serious about this. I don't like it and I don't want to hear it anymore. The next person who says anything prejudicial is out. Okay, let's go on. Maura, I'd like you to do 'I Get a Kick Out of You.' Try it from the platform."

Stimpson had had Eben build a special platform several feet above stage level. It had a railing around it, making it like a ship's deck. Maura walked up the ramp which led from stage to platform and waited for Alan to start the music. We were all sitting in the audience quietly, anxiously, because this was the first time Maura had sung the song. She started, staring out above our heads, but when she got to the words, "I suddenly turn and see your fabulous face," she turned her head and looked directly at Phil, who was sitting by himself in the first row. Maura sang the whole song to Phil. Every body tried to contain their laughter because they didn't want Stimpson to stop the song. Even Maura had to fight to keep from breaking up. From where I was sitting I could see that Phil's neck was turning a bright red. Somehow, I didn't think it was too funny. I looked at Janet and Mary El and saw that they weren't laughing either. But everyone else was . . . except, of course, for Jeff, who got up in the middle of the song and walked to the back of the theater.

When Maura finished everybody burst into applause. And then the most peculiar thing happened. Phil rose to his feet and applauded louder and longer than anyone else. When the rest of the kids stopped clapping, Phil went on for a few seconds longer. Then he yelled up to Maura.

"Thank you, Maura, that was lovely. It's been a long time since anyone sang to me. I appreciate it."

His voice wavered slightly and when he turned around to walk to the back of the theater, I could see that, as nonchalant as he tried to be, the muscles in his cheeks were jumping and his eyes were narrowed and hurt.

Stimpson walked over to us.

"Janet," she said, "what's going on tonight?"

"What do you mean?"

"I think you know. What was that all about?"

"You mean Maura's singing to Phil? I don't know . . . maybe she's got a thing for him."

Stimpson stared at her for a moment with obvious disbelief and then walked to the back of the theater.

"Do you think Jeff and Phil will tell her?" Mary El said.

"Of course not," Janet said. "It's bad enough *we* know . . . you think they want an adult to know?"

After rehearsal I got Mary El to drop me off right away. I didn't want to go out with the kids because I wanted to get to my reading on homosexuality.

Mother and Ray were sitting on the porch when I got home and I rapped with them a few minutes. Then I said I was tired, which I was, and went up-stairs.

It would be impossible for me to write down here everything about homosexuality that's in Dr. Reuben's book . . . and anyway, what would be the point? So I'll just give you some key sentences.

What is male homosexuality? . . . They often transform themselves into part-time women. Do all homosexuals act this way? . . . Most homosexuals at one time or another act out some aspect of the female role. Would Jeff do that? Phil? I couldn't picture it.

What do homosexuals really do with each other? After describing mutual masturbation Dr. Reuben says: *Three to five minutes should be enough for*

the entire operation. Three to five minutes? How
could that be possible? I was beginning to feel really
sick. *Surely there must be more to homosexuality? A
homosexual may have as many as five sexual experi-
ences in one evening—all with different partners. He
rarely knows their names.* Well, that certainly wasn't
true about Jeff and Phil . . . or were there other boys
involved? Boys they didn't know? I was getting more
and more confused. The words whirled by me.

Aren't homosexuals afraid *of being arrested?* Dr.
Reuben says no . . . they like danger. *But* all *homosexuals aren't like that, are they? Unfortunately, they
are just like that.* Maybe Jeff and Phil weren't homosexuals after all. There were other questions and answers about homosexual language and sexual activity
—each paragraph more depressing than the last.

And then, finally: *Basically all homosexuals are
alike . . . looking for love where there can be no
love and looking for sexual satisfaction where there
can be no lasting satisfaction.* Why? Why could there
be no love? I couldn't understand that. Jeff had said
he and Phil loved each other. But then Jeff was very
young and Dr. Reuben was a doctor, after all. He
should know. Besides, would they publish a book that
wasn't true? Oh, poor Jeff, poor Phil. They didn't know
how miserable they were. They thought they loved
each other and they couldn't . . . they were sick, awful
people. Janet was right: The best thing to do was to
stay away from them. I was very glad I wasn't a boy
because if I was maybe they'd try and get me to . . .

There was a knock on my door. Mother came in. I
was glad I had put the book away because I didn't
want Mother to ask me questions right at that moment.
Not that she censored my reading—quite the con-
trary. She said I should real everything and anything.
But she probably would want to discuss the book or
ask why I had chosen it and I didn't feel like going
into that."

"Jeff's downstairs," she said.

"Huh?"

"Jeff. He's downstairs. He said he wanted to talk with you . . . it's important."

How could I talk to him? How could I even look at him? Jeff was a pervert—a degenerate. If Mother knew that she probably wouldn't even want him in the house. "Tell him I'm asleep," I said.

"Have you and Jeff had a fight?"

"I don't feel like talking about it."

"Okay." She started to leave, then turned. "Camilla, you know how I feel about privacy and I don't mean to interfere—whatever has happened between you and Jeff is your business. But he *does* seem terribly upset. And you *have* been good friends for years. Are you sure you won't see him?"

"What do you mean, terribly upset?"

"Kind of twitchy . . . nervous. I can't be sure but he may have been crying—his eyes are all red."

Jeff crying. Maybe he was getting more feminine already. Oh, no, now I was getting stupid. I knew better than that. There was nothing wrong with boys crying and one of the things I had always liked about Jeff was that he wasn't afraid to cry. We'd often shared a Kleenex in a movie. Jeff had been a good friend to me and I guessed that I owed him at least one last conversation. "Okay . . . tell him I'll be down in a sec."

It was a beautiful night. The moon was full and it lit up the water and the beach as if we'd turned on floodlights. Jeff and I didn't say anything as we walked down the path to the beach. I sat on the sand and watched as he shakily lit one of his Marlboros. Then he sat down, facing me.

"I'm sorry if I got you out of bed," he said.

"That's okay."

"I thought it was important that we talk."

"What about?" I realized we had switched our usual roles.

"You know what about, Camel."

When he called me Camel I felt like bursting into tears and throwing my arms around him. I guess it brought back all the close times we had had in the past. Then I remembered the facts. Aside from everything else, Jeff had taken Phil away from me.

"First of all," he said, clearing his throat, "I want to tell you about Phil and me."

"You don't have to," I said. "I know all about it."

"No, you don't."

"Yes, I do. No, I don't. Which one of you is the girl?"

"What?" He sounded genuinely shocked.

"You heard me."

"Where did you get that crap?"

"Look, Jeff," I said, trying to sound very knowledgeable, "I know a great deal about the subject of homosexuality."

"Really?"

"Yes."

"I doubt it."

I started to rise. "Well, if you're going to be like that . . ."

"Don't," he said, gently pushing me down. "Don't let's get into dramatics."

"Then don't get snotty."

"I'm sorry . . . I really am. But when you say a thing like Which one of you is the girl . . . well, I can't help it. It isn't like that. I have no interest in being a girl and neither does Phil. I mean, if we wanted girls—well—we'd be with girls, wouldn't we?"

That did seem logical.

"I guess I should start at the beginning."

"You don't have to."

"I want to."

He was silent and kicked at the sand.

"Well, go ahead," I said.

"This isn't easy for me." He lit one cigarette from another. "Okay . . . well, a couple of years ago when I wasn't too interested in girls it didn't bother me much. I mean lots of guys are more interested in sports and stuff when they're thirteen and fourteen; but by the time I was sixteen and I still couldn't see what all the fuss was about, I guess I got worried. Also I was very aware that I had crushes on guys—especially Mr. Safier. I knew I was a little too old for that."

"Just last year I had a crush on Mrs. Violett but that doesn't mean I'm . . ."

"Did you think about her sexually?"

"No."

"Well, that's the difference. I did. Anyway, I knew something was different about me but I didn't want to face it so that's when I started going out with Tina. Well, you know what a bust that was."

"But Jeff, we talked about that. You know that happens to lots of boys."

"Oh, Camilla. I couldn't do it because I didn't want to. I wasn't interested. I mean . . . well, I know how this is going to sound to you but . . . well . . . it just didn't seem natural to me."

"Maybe it was because Tina's not your type."

"And Sue, and Debbie and all the others I could've gone out with? No . . . it's *girls* who aren't my type. I mean, I *like* girls, but they just don't turn me on—sexually. Boys do."

"All boys?" I asked, remembering Dr. Reuben.

"Of course not. Do all boys turn you on?"

"No."

"Well, it's no different. What I mean is that all boys don't turn me on any more than all girls would turn me on if I dug them."

"Why? Why is it boys instead of girls?"

"I really don't know, but it doesn't matter."

"What do you mean? Of course it matters," I said.

"No, it really doesn't. Let me tell you about Joe Martin. Joe is a senior at Phil's college and is living in East Hampton this summer. Phil and I went to see him . . . he's a really terrific guy. Anyway, he talked to us about the whole thing and he said a lot of things that made sense."

"Like what?"

"Well, for instance that it really doesn't matter *why* we're the way we are as long as it doesn't make us unhappy. He says that all the talk about parents

and environment or genetics or whatever being the
cause of homosexuality is for the birds. He says the
only thing that matters is caring for and respecting
someone."

"Why can't you care for and respect a girl, Jeff?"

"Because it just doesn't do it for me. I don't know
why. That's just the way it is. Another thing Joe says
is that being different doesn't make you special; it's
just being different, that's all. He says a lot of people
won't understand that and will try to change you,
but you've got to stand up for what you are: A person
has the right to be anything he or she wants. Maybe
you should meet Joe."

"Is he . . . is he a . . . ?"

"Homosexual? Yes."

"Well, then what do you expect? Naturally he'd defend it." It sounded to me like Jeff had been sold a
bill of goods.

"Look, Camilla—the point is I don't think I was
ever really happy until I met Phil."

"Love at first sight," I said snidely.

"Please don't," he said softly.

"I'm sorry," I said. I was.

"But, as a matter of fact, no. . . . If you remember,
I couldn't stand him. I guess it was because somewhere I was attracted to him and didn't even know
it. I saw something in him and it scared me. That's
why I was acting so crazy with you and everything.
Camilla, the one thing I'm really sorry about is that
you dug him."

"I love him," I said.

"I really feel bad about that—honestly. I wish it
could have been someone else. But . . . well, Phil
never could have returned your love, even if he
hadn't met *me*."

"Then why did he take me out?"

"Because he was trying to fight it just like I was."

"Well, why did he come to the barbecue?"

"Because he was still trying to fight it. We both
tried, Cam. As much for you as for ourselves. But

we love each other . . . we just couldn't fight it. I've
never been myself before—and I've never been so
happy in all my life. The only thing I'm unhappy
about is that you had to get hurt."

"Jeff," I said, "don't you know you're looking for
love where there can be no love?"

He looked at me a moment and then started laughing. I hadn't heard Jeff laugh so hard in ages. "Godal-
mighty, Cam, you sound like something out of a soap
opera. Where'd you get that?"

I have to admit I felt a little foolish. Jeff seemed
so cool and here I was coming on like . . . like what?
Who could I trust if I couldn't trust a published
author and doctor? "Jeff . . . I do have some interest
in you, you know, and I did some reading and . . ."

"Who'd you read?" he said, laughing again. "Dr.
Reuben?"

Do you know what it feels like when a thing like
that happens? I mean, do you know how you wish
that the sea would open up and swallow you? Or
that the feared hydrogen bomb would be dropped
at that very second? I mean, what could I say? No,
I never heard of Doctor Reuben. Doctor Reuben
who? Well, the only thing you can do—the only
thing I could do was to sit up very straight, look him
directly in the eye and as sound pompous as possible.

"Exactly. Dr. David Reuben was Chief of Neuro-
psychiatry at Walker Air Force Base Hospital and a
clinical research associate at Harvard, and is now
a practicing psychiatrist."

"And a shmuck," Jeff said.

"I suppose you know more about things than he
does?"

"Camilla, Reuben is a jerk. Did you read the whole
book?"

I shook my head.

"Well, if you read the whole book you'll find that
the very things he says can't be satisfying sexually
for homosexuals are the same things he says are fine
and satisfying for heterosexuals. I mean it just doesn't

make sense. Anyway, he wrote the book to make a lot of bread—and he did—but nobody takes him seriously. He's misinformed."

"How do you know?"

"I know. Do you think I'm insane? Do you?"

"What are you talking about?"

"Just answer me."

"No, of course not."

"Okay. Well, unless I'm crazy I *am* being satisfied —emotionally and sexually."

"But it's wrong, Jeff."

"Who says so?"

"Everybody knows that."

"How? How does it hurt you? . . . Well, you're not a good example at this point. Okay, how does it hurt Janet, or Sam or Walt or anybody else if Phil and I love each other? How?"

I didn't know how to answer him. Logically, he was right. It didn't hurt anyone else . . . not really. Yet it was wrong. It had to be wrong. Didn't it? I felt very confused and tired all at once. I stood up. "I have to go to sleep, Jeff."

He rose too. "You can't answer that, can you?"

"I just know it's wrong."

"You're really rigid, you know that? I mean, why does everything always have to be the same?"

"What do you mean?"

"I mean love. Like Joe says, does it always have to be wrapped up in the same size package with the same color bow? As long as people love instead of hate, what difference does it make who they love?"

"I just don't think you're seeing things clearly," I said.

"I guess one of us isn't."

I turned and started up the path toward the house.

"Camilla? What are your plans? What are the kids planning to do? I mean, I know we're getting the silent treatment and remarks and stuff like Maura's lousy performance tonight, but is that all? Is that all that's going to happen?"

"I don't know."

"Because it doesn't matter to me—I can take it. But Phil . . . well, I'm not so sure about him. He's very sensitive and he's more uptight about it all than I am."

"You mean he *knows* it's wrong."

"Go to hell, Camilla."

We both turned away at the same time and I walked up the path, never looking back. I wondered if that was the last thing Jeff Grathwohl would ever say to me.

"Did you have a good talk?" Mother asked, when I opened the porch door.

"It was okay," I said. "Mother, did you ever read Dr. Reuben's book?"

"You mean *Everything You*—"

"Yes."

"I looked it over. Why?"

"Would you say it was a good book or what?"

"Trash," she said. "It was written to make a buck, that's all."

"Thanks."

"Is Jeff trying to get you to read it?"

"Hardly. He said it was trash, too."

"Jeff's a bright boy."

I wanted to say, "And he's a faggot, too," but I didn't. I just said good night.

I thought about all the things Jeff had said to me and I tried to understand, but I knew that no matter what I thought, I'd go along with the rest of the kids. I just didn't have the courage to stick my neck out for Jeff and Phil, no matter what. Besides, I still thought it was wrong.

As long as people love instead of hate, what difference does it make who they love? I couldn't stop hearing those words. It did seem to make some kind of sense. So what? Everybody knew gay people were creeps. But even if Phil was a creep—a creepy queer—I still loved him. I loved him and he could never be mine. I'd lost Phil forever. I thought about his sweet kiss. Oh, Phil. Maybe it was just a phase. I tried to console myself with that for about five minutes but it just didn't go down. Jeff and Phil loved each other . . . or so they thought. Now I was really confused. I mean, now I didn't even have Reuben's confusing ideas to go by. Maybe I should talk to Mother. But I knew I wasn't quite ready for that, just as I knew that I would talk to her about it sometime.

When I look back on that decision now—the decision to put off talking with Mother—I wonder if I'd talked with her then . . . and understood things the way I do now . . . I wonder if two lives might have been saved. But there's no way I'll ever know that, and no use in regretting. I'll just have to live with it the rest of my life and hope that maybe I learned something.

Chapter 17

~~~~~~~~~~~~~~~~~~~~~~~~~~~~~~~~

Well nothing much happened for the next few weeks.
But the show started to take shape. The sets got
built in spite of Eben and the costumes were being
made and my two dances and songs started to come
together, and now everybody was on stage almost
every night. Some nights it felt like it was going to
be good and some nights it seemed like a disaster
. . . but Stimpson encouraged us and said it was always
like that.

As for Jeff and Phil, the kids made fun of them a
lot and started referring to them as Skinny and
Booby, respectively. Jeff and I never spoke and he
didn't seem to mind too much that he had become
an outcast. But Phil showed signs of nervousness.
He had begun to smoke and I noticed that he was
biting his nails.

I hadn't gotten over Phil but I guess you could
say that I was learning to live with it. I went out
with Walt a few times but it really didn't mean anything because we had known each other for a long
time. I missed Jeff a lot but I didn't know what to do
about it.

Mother and Ray saw each other every weekend
and Rachel had started spending all her time with
Kurt Binns.

Janet had fallen in love with Maura's brother Jim
and so had about five other girls. He really was the

neatest-looking boy around and if I hadn't been so heartbroken I probably could have worked up an interest in him myself. At the moment he seemed interested in Penny, who couldn't make up her mind between Jim and Todd Breese, the drummer in our four-piece band. So far the band stank and was constantly throwing everybody off, but we had hopes for them.

Tina and Eben were still an item and Mary El was still mooning over Sam, who was still mooning over his older woman, Linda.

The show was to open on August eighth and everything went along all right until Monday, the sixth; then, I guess you could safely say, all hell began to break loose.

A work party to clean the theater had been scheduled for seven thirty and our third run-through was to be at eight thirty. We'd had our first dress the previous Friday and, naturally, it had been a disaster. It was a good thing we had the weekend to get over it. Stimpson had put Janet in charge of the work party. We all agreed it would be good for morale if Alan and Connie stayed at the piano and played while we cleaned. They started playing songs from *South Pacific* and the kids who'd been in last year's show sang along with the piano while they worked.

Before I tell you what happened, I should explain that it's a practice, or tradition, for the kids to change the titles and words of the songs in a given show. For instance, "Anything Goes" has been changed to "Anything Gross!" "It's Delovely" was "It's Disgusting" and "Let's Misbehave" was . . . well, I'll leave that one to your imagination!

So when Alan started playing "Younger Than Springtime" from *S.P.*, nobody was surprised that Walt jumped up on the stage with a broom and told everyone to hold it.

"I have it," he said. "Professor, start the music again."

Walt held out the broom and looked at it longingly. Then he began to sing in his croaky voice.

"Gayer than springtime are you, Sweeter than music are you, Angel and lover, heaven and earth are you to Jeff. Gayer than springtime is Jeff, Feyer than laughter is Jeff, Angel and lover, heaven and earth is Jeff to Phil!"

Everybody started roaring with laughter and then Walt jumped off the stage, ran over to where Phil was stuffing some garbage into a plastic sack, and began singing the same lyrics to him. Phil tried to ignore him but no matter which way he turned Walt got in front of him. I could see that Phil was turning red and the muscles in his cheeks were jumping faster and faster. Suddenly, he dropped the sack and took a swing at Walt, who ducked.

"No," Jeff yelled and came running down the aisle toward them. Somebody stuck a foot out and Jeff went flying but caught onto a chair so he didn't hit the floor. Harlan and Eben rushed toward Walt and Phil from the back of the theater but Jeff got there first and stepped between them.

"Cool it . . . c'mon . . . cool it, you guys."

"I'll kill him," Phil said in a tight, strangled voice.

"No . . . no, Phil—don't . . . don't give in to them. They're stupid."

"I don't care. I can't stand it."

"C'mon," Eben said, "let the little faggot punk alone —he's gonna break down and cry any minute now. We've got more important things to do than messing with screwed-up queers."

Walt nodded and walked away. Phil was still shaking with rage and Jeff guided him outside.

By the time Stimpson arrived, things were okay except that Maura hadn't shown up. Nobody had noticed during the work party because I guess nobody expected Maura to help with that, even though it said on the schedule that there were to be no exceptions. We had all gotten used to the fact that

Maura *was* an exception. It was funny that none of us resented it but maybe that was because we could see that Maura was special. At least her talent was special. There wasn't a person in the company who didn't think, know, believe that she would be a big star someday. It wasn't that she thought she was better than we were or anything—it was just that she was kind of high-strung and she did have a heavy burden. I mean, she really had to carry the show. So when she wasn't there by quarter of nine and Janet couldn't get any answer at her house, Stimpson said we'd do the run-through with Penny. Naturally, Penny was hysterical. She hadn't had much rehearsal but she was supposed to watch everything Maura did so she'd know the part. Penny had been pretty sure Maura would never miss a performance so she really hadn't paid very close attention. She knew the lines and the words to the songs . . . but the dances were another matter.

Of course, with Penny playing Reno Sweeney, there were only three Angels.

"What'll we do about Penny's part, Susan?" Janet asked Stimpson.

"I guess we'll have to go with three Angels and take that adjustment," Stimpson said.

"Excuse me," said Lillian. She was a summer resident and none of us knew her too well. "I've been watching carefully and I think I could do Penny's part—I mean, just as a fill-in."

So she became the fourth Angel. The first act went okay but, as hard as Penny tried, it was obvious to all of us that she was no Maura. On the other hand, Lillian was a really good Angel. It was amazing how much she knew.

At the beginning of the second act everybody but Walt and Eben was onstage and we could hear a commotion somewhere backstage. From where I was standing I could see Janet and Phil kind of wrestling with someone but I couldn't see who it was.

Then it was time for one of my numbers, "Let's Step Out." I got through it all right but I knew it wasn't good. During "Let's Misbehave," which Sam and Penny did, the rest of us had to freeze so I couldn't see anything in the wings. But I could hear muffled voices. Fortunately, they didn't carry into the orchestra so Stimpson didn't know anything was going on.

I wasn't on at the beginning of Scene 2 so I quickly went backstage to see what was happening. No one was there. I figured Phil, Janet, and the mysterious third person had gone outside and I was right. I saw them across the street and ran over. Janet and Phil were with a very drunken Maura.

"Oh, wow," I said.

"Wow isn't the word for it," Janet said.

"What happened?"

"She got drunk," Phil said.

"Thanks," I said, "I can see that."

"Well," Maura said, "if it isn't little Bonnie. Hey, Bonnie, tell these creeps I have to go on."

I looked at Janet.

"She wants to go on."

"Penny Lademan can't do my part," Maura slurred. "She's second-rate and you know it."

"Yeah, well, tonight you'd be fourth rate," Phil said.

"Shut up, fag," Maura said.

And Phil slapped her across the face, "Oh, God," he said immediately. "I'm sorry . . . I'm really sorry, Maura—I . . . oh, God." He covered his face with his hands and Maura was free on one side.

She quickly wriggled away from Janet's hold and started running across the street toward the theater.

"Get her," Janet yelled. "We can't let Stimpson see her like that."

We both ran after her and I grabbed her on the steps of the theater. Several chorus kids were there and one of them said I was on in a couple of seconds.

I yelled for Sam and he took Maura back across the street with Janet.

I went on, did my little bit, and then raced back outside and across the street. The kids had Maura in her car.

"What's happening?" I asked.

"Hank ... I want Hank," Maura said.

"She wants Hank," Janet said, rolling her eyes. "I think she broke up with him or something."

"He broke up with me. He said everybody's sheep ... even he's sheep."

"Sheep?"

"Who knows?" said Sam.

"Look," Janet said, "you two get back on stage for the last scene and Phil and I will stay with her. When rehearsal's over Phil can drive Maura's car and you guys can follow in Mary El's. And tell those chorus kids to keep their mouths shut. This we don't want Stimpson to know. Tell her I got sick and Phil drove me home."

Phil was sitting in the back seat, staring straight ahead, and I desperately wanted to say something to him, but I couldn't think of anything to say so I just walked back to the theater with Sam.

When rehearsal was over, Mary El, Walt, Sam, and I got in Mary El's car and followed the others to Maura's house in Greenport. Fortunately, her parents were out. Janet, Mary El, and I got her in the house and up to her room. We undressed her and put her to bed. Then we got out of there as fast as we could.

Back in Mary El's car, I sat between Walt and Phil. It was the first time Phil had been with any of us since it all happened. You could feel the tension in the car like a seventh person.

On the way back toward the theater we talked about Maura and Hank and wondered if she would come through all right now that he'd broken up with her. Everyone decided that, basically, Maura was a pro and it was better that this had happened now than on opening night. Phil said nothing. When we hit the light in Southold a car full of kids pulled up next to us. They honked the horn.

"Hey, we're going to Kenny's Beach," Todd Breese yelled. "They got Jeff Grathwohl up there and they're gonna teach that fag a lesson." They pulled away.

"Oh, my God," Phil said.

"Hurry, Mary El," I said.

As she turned up Youngs Avenue, everybody was talking at once.

"What did he mean?"

"Oh, my God."

"Who's got him?"

"Poor Jeff."

"We've got to help him."

"It's too much."

"Oh, my God."

"Gross."

"Barbaric."

When we turned onto Soundview we could see three cars aheads of us going toward Kenny's. Phil just kept saying "Oh, my God" over and over again. Even before we hit the parking lot we heard the noise and shouts. Some kids were 360-degreeing it (that's when you race forward in your car and suddenly brake and go around in a 360-degree turn . . . usually with a bottle or a person on the roof of the car . . . something none of us ever did) and we swerved to get out of the way. Mary El jammed on her brakes and we all jumped out.

Someone yelled that they were on the beach and we started running. We could see a fire about a thousand feet away and a bunch of kids standing by it. I've never run so fast in my life.

The first person I recognized was Eben. He was standing with his arms across his naked chest, staring down at the ground. Then I saw Bruce and Harlan. There were some kids from the chorus and a lot of kids I didn't recognize. They were forming a circle and I had to push two kids aside to see what was in the middle. I almost fainted.

There was Jeff, lying on his back, a gag in his mouth, in his underwear. He was spread-eagled and his wrists and ankles were tied to some posts that had been pounded deep into the sand.

Phil smashed through the circle and Eben and Harlan grabbed him, pinning his arms behind him.

"You want the same, queer?"

"Let me go . . . let me go," he shouted.

Eben smacked him across the mouth and told him to shut up.

"Stop it," I yelled.

"Oh, your old girlfriend wants us to stop," Eben said. Then he turned to me. "You keep out of this, Camilla."

"I won't," I said.

"No? What are you going to do about it?"

I started to open my mouth but realized I was helpless. I turned to Walt and Sam. "Help them," I said.

"There's too many of them," Sam said quietly.

"Hey, guys," Walt said, "a joke's a joke but . . ."

"Shut up," Eben said.

Someone had to stop them. I looked around for Tina but she wasn't there. It was hopeless—we couldn't fight them. Sam was right . . . we were outnumbered.

The beach was filling up with every passing minute. It was always the same. No one ever really understood how the word spread when there was something going on, but it did. It was as though there were a secret underground and someone tapped out Morse-code messages to all parts of the North Fork. The kids would come from as far up as Orient and as far down as Mattituck. At the moment, there was a group of boys from East Marion who were joining the circle. There was no way to know where anyone stood—which side they'd be on.

"Maybe those guys will help," I said to Sam, pointing to the boys from East Marion.

"Why should they?" Sam said.

"I don't know . . . couldn't we ask them?"

"Nobody wants to help," Walt said. "They just want to watch."

I knew he was right. I felt desperate and started searching the faces around me, looking for something —some sign that someone might help. Then I saw a new group pushing its way to the front of the circle and any shred of hope I'd had was demolished. It was Hank Allen and a bunch of black jocks from Greenport. What could be sweeter to them than to see one of us hurt? If anyone had been willing to help before, surely they wouldn't if they had to fight Hank and his friends. I started to tell Janet that it was hopeless now but she was opening her mouth to speak.

"Just what do you plan to do, Eben?" she asked in her cool way.

"We're gonna mete out a punishment worthy of the crime," he said.

"And what crime is that?"

"A crime against nature," he said.

"Oh, come on, Eben . . ."

"It's screwed up—they're screwed up. They deserve what they get."

"They don't hurt you," I shouted.

"They offend my senses," he said. "Where are those jerks with the stuff?"

"Here they come," Harlan yelled.

We all turned to look. Coming down the beach were four guys rolling a big metal can. A fifth boy was carrying a white sack.

I turned back toward Phil and saw that they'd put a gag in his mouth and that Todd and Bruce were holding him.

"Janet," I whispered. "Hank Allen and his friends are here . . . there's no hope now."

"I know," she said.

"Should one of us go for the police?"

"I don't know . . . I don't think so. The whole thing might come out and Jeff's and Phil's parents . . . Oh, God—no, no police."

"Well, what are we gonna do—just watch?"

"I don't know. I have to think."

Just then the guys with the can and sack reached the group.

"Okay, good," Eben said. "Open it up." He turned toward Jeff. "Now what we got here, Grathwohl," he said, patting the can, "is some nice fresh, black, gooey, smelly tar."

Some of the kids gasped and Phil struggled but couldn't pull free of Todd and Bruce.

Eben went on. "And what we got here," he said, pointing to the white sack, "is a bag of freshly plucked pillow feathers."

"You can't do this, Eben," I yelled, rushing over to him.

"No? And who's gonna stop me? You? Those creeps you hang around with? The Jew and the Bore? Get out of the way, Camilla." He gave me a slight push, and Walt and Sam came into the center of the circle and led me back.

"We've got to get the police," I said, beginning to cry.

"I just don't know," Janet said.

"Now what we're gonna do," Eben said, "is we're gonna make you nice and black . . ."

"Black like me?" Hank Allen said.

"Hey, man, what do ya say?" Eben said, and put out his hand.

Hank didn't take it. He looked down at Jeff a minute and shook his head.

"What the hell is this, man?"

"This guy's queer," Eben said, pointing at Jeff. "We're gonna give him a little lesson."

"Yeah? What lesson's that?"

"We're gonna tar and feather him. We got his faggy friend over there." He pointed at Phil.

"Then you gonna tar and feather him, too?"

"Yeah. Ya wanna help, man?"

Slowly Hank shook his head back and forth, his hands on his hips. "Man, you honkies is screwed up good. Who is this guy?" He pointed at Jeff.

"He's Jeff Grathwohl," I said. "He's a friend of Maura's." I hoped Maura had told Hank about the night when Jeff came to her rescue.

"Jeff Grathwohl," Hank said, slowly. "Yeah, I remember that name."

"Come on," Eben said. "Let's get going."

Nobody moved.

"Now, just hold on here a minute," Hank said. "I wanna get this thing straight in my head. This Grathwohl dude and this other dude over there are queers, right?"

"Right," Eben said.

"And you're gonna tar and feather them, right?"

"Right."

"Why?" Hank asked.

"What do you mean, why? I just told ya—they're fags."

"They been rapin' you or somethin'?"

There were some titters and I could see that Eben was starting to lose his cool.

"Are you kidding? I'd kill 'em if they so much as touched me."

"Yeah? What are you afraid of, huh?"

"Afraid of? Man, you must be crazy," Eben said.

"Well, if you ain't afraid of them, what you got to kill 'em for?"

"They're screwed up," Eben said.

"Yeah. Maybe so. But what's that got to do with you, huh?"

Eben shifted his weight from one foot to the other and folded his arms across his chest. "Whatsa matter, Allen? You like queers or something?"

Hank stared at Eben a second and shook his head in that slow way again. "More sheep," he said.

Janet and I looked at each other, remembering Maura's muttering.

"What we got here," Hank said, "is a bunch a white sheep and a bunch a black sheep."

My heart was making a racket inside me. Was it possible that Hank was going to help?

"So, I repeat, honkie: What's it got to do with you? Unless, maybe you're afraid you can't resist one of these boys, huh?"

The crowd laughed.

"You shut your goddamn black mouth," Eben shouted.

It was as though Eben had slapped everyone across the face, the way the silence fell. Nobody moved and all eyes were on Hank. A muscle twitched in his cheek and then, very slowly, he smiled.

"Well, well . . . it looks like I scored a point."

"Are you callin' me a fag?" Eben said.

"I'm just wonderin' what you're so afraid of, that's all. Now the fact that these two boys are queer don't scare me none. They scare you, Cal?"

"Oh, yeah. They make me shake all over, Hank," a tall skinny black boy said, laughing.

"How about you?" Hank asked another one of his friends.

"I'm prayin' for my life," he answered.

"Me, too," another one said.

"They gonna get me like the plague."

"Now, you see what I mean, white boy?"

Eben's face seemed to grow red even in the dim light of the fire and the veins around his temples looked like they might burst. "Listen, you dumb jock," he yelled, "I got hundreds of chicks I make it with so you just shut your mouth. I dig chicks, you get it? Chicks, chicks, chicks—that's all I care about. I can't get enough of them . . . you get it?" he screamed.

"Sure—sure I get it. You got chicks comin' out your ears, right?"

"Right. Now why don't you just buzz off, 'cause this is none of your business. C'mon, guys."

He motioned to Harlan and his other cronies and started toward the can of tar.

"Hold it," Hank said.

"Butt out," Eben said.

"Listen, honkie, you're a screwed-up son of a bitch and I don't like you, but you get your ass out of here now and I'll forget all about this little incident. You dig?"

"This isn't your fight, man. How come you're messin' in here?"

" 'Cause I don't like sheep."

"But you like faggots?"

"Not particularly . . . but they don't bother me, I don't bother them. Everybody don't swing the same way, man, and the sooner you get that through your pretty ofay head, the better off you'll be."

"Like you, huh? You swing with white chicks, right?"

"People is people, ya know? There's good people and bad people . . . you're bad people. Now get your ass off this beach before I get real mad."

"Even your own people don't like you runnin' with white chicks."

"Even blacks got bad people, man. Shove off."

Then Hank walked over and pulled the gag out of Jeff's mouth and untied his wrists. Slowly, Jeff sat up and started untying his ankles. I looked around for his clothes and saw them lying in a heap near the water. When I gave them to him he nodded and started to dress.

Hank turned around and looked at Eben, who was glaring at him. "Oh, you still here? I guess this dude wants to be escorted." He nodded toward some of his friends and they started walking toward Eben.

Eben began backing up. "Okay—okay . . . I'm goin'."

Todd and Bruce let go of Phil and everybody started moving down the beach toward the cars.

When Jeff was dressed he walked over to Hank. "Thanks," he said.

"I owed you one," said Hank. Then he turned and

started walking away with his friends. "Man, nobody lets nobody live," he said, to no one in particular.

We watched them disappear into the dark and then we were alone—Janet, Walt, Sam, Mary El, Phil, Jeff, and me.

"C'mon," Mary El said to Phil and Jeff, "we'll drive you back to your cars."

We started up the beach, each of us thinking about what had almost happened and what *had* happened. And I suppose the others, like me, were thinking that the worst was over . . . nothing as awful as this night could happen again.

Chapter 18

On Tuesday Maura asked me to have lunch with her. We ate late so the Sweet Shop was reasonably empty when we got there. It was unusual for Maura to have lunch out and even more unusual for her to have lunch with me. In fact, you could say it was a first. But when we sat down in the booth I found out why.

"I want to thank you for last night," she said.

"That's okay."

"No, I really appreciate it. I could have blown the whole thing if it hadn't been for you and the other kids. So have anything you want—this is on me."

"You don't have to do that, Maura."

"I want to."

I shrugged and thanked her. We ordered and then I asked her why she had gotten drunk.

"Hank and I broke up, and I guess . . . I don't know—isn't that what people do when they break up?"

"What people?"

"I don't know. People in the movies, I guess."

"I guess. How come you broke up?"

"Pressure. Hank couldn't take it anymore. He said he hated himself for doing it—you know, for giving in like that—but he couldn't stand what was happening to me and to him. He said we're all a bunch of sheep."

"Tell me about the sheep thing," I said.

"Well, he said people are just like sheep. Everybody

has to be the same. The minute anybody does something different from the rest of the crowd—whatever crowd they're part of—then they're outcasts. He said it was a rare person who could take that kind of pressure and he was ashamed of himself but he couldn't take it. He said he was a sheep, just like all the rest."

"I saw him last night," I said, and told Maura what had happened.

"I guess now you know why I love him. He's a neat guy."

Our food came and we started eating. We didn't say anything for a few minutes. Then something occurred to me.

"So what it comes down to is that you and Hank can't be together because other people don't like it, right?"

"That's the way it bounces," she said.

"It's really the same thing as Jeff and Phil, isn't it?"

"Are you kidding? Jeff and Phil are queers."

"Yes, I know, but . . ."

"I don't see how you can compare us."

"But I can," I said. "You and Hank have to break up because other people don't like it, right?"

"Right."

"Well, other people don't like the idea of Jeff and Phil together and . . ."

"But that's different," she said.

"How?"

"Because Hank and I are normal. I mean, Hank is black and I'm white but at least what we feel for each other is normal . . . healthy."

"A lot of people don't think so, Maura. If everybody thought it was normal or so healthy you wouldn't be in this predicament."

"Well, it's just different from Jeff and Phil," she said irritably. "You can't compare them."

But somehow, I thought you could. I wasn't sure how or exactly what I was getting at. I just knew things

were beginning to come together—to click into place—
and that something was really wrong with the way all
of us had been acting. Not just Eben. He was worse
than the rest, but all of us were screwed up about this
thing.

"I'm sorry about you and Hank," I said. "If two
people love each other they should be together, no
matter what."

"That's what I think."

"Do you?"

"Huh?"

"Jeff and Phil love each other."

She looked at me a minute, her sandwich halfway
to her mouth. She put it back on the plate. "Do you
think they really do?"

"They say they do. Why shouldn't we believe it?"

"Yeah, I guess." A few seconds passed. "I don't know,
Camilla . . . I mean, I see what you're getting at, but
something about it just won't go down."

"I guess that's what people feel about you and Hank.
It just won't go down."

We looked at each other for what seemed a long
time and then I saw tears in Maura's eyes. She didn't
try to hide them or even wipe at them when they
started down her cheeks. And even though, when she
started to talk, she went back to Hank I knew I had
gotten to her just a little.

"I guess it won't go down for Hank either," she said.
"I mean, he just can't hack it. He's really special to
his people, you know. I mean they practically think
he's a saint or something because he's such a big jock
and he's won all those trophies and everything. I
guess when you're important you gotta make certain
sacrifices."

"I guess," I said. But I didn't really believe it. It
seemed to me that no matter who you were you
shouldn't have to do things just to please other people—not if what you wanted didn't really hurt anyone else. And that was it, wasn't it? Jeff had said it.

How does it hurt Janet or Sam or Walt or anybody else if Phil and I love each other? The truth was, it didn't. Well, yes, in this particular case, I had been hurt. But not because Phil and Jeff were homosexuals.

Maura and I finished lunch and went back to our A&P WEO life. I looked for Sam during our break because I wanted to talk to him about Jeff and Phil and the way we'd all been acting, but he wasn't around.

When we finished work and were standing outside waiting for Mrs. Ahlers, I broached the subject.

"Sam, I think what's been going on with Phil and Jeff is terrible."

"What's new about that?"

"No, I mean, what we've . . ."

And then his mother drove up and, of course, we couldn't continue the conversation. That was my first blundering attempt to try and right what I now thought was a terrible wrong. When Mrs. Ahlers dropped me off at my driveway, I crossed through the yard and went to Jeff's house. I had to talk to him. I had to let him know that even though I didn't understand completely, I knew I had been behaving terribly and it would be different from now on . . . or something like that. His car wasn't there but that didn't necessarily mean he wasn't home. The Dragon Lady sometimes used his car. But not this time.

"Oh, hello, Camilla," the D.L. said when she saw me standing there.

"Hello. Is Jeff home?"

"No."

"Is he coming home for dinner?"

"I'm not sure that's any of your business," she said. "Jeffrey leads his own life, you know."

"It's important that I talk to him." I was trying to keep my cool, but it took everything I had not to come right out and tell her what I thought of her.

"Well, he's not here. You know, my dear, you shouldn't chase boys."

That really burned me up. "Jeff and I are friends—
I'm not chasing him. I just want to talk with him, not
sleep with him."

Slam! The door closed in my face. Okay, I'd talk
to Jeff at the theater.

Mother was in New York seeing patients, so Rachel
and I had the pleasure of each other's company at
dinner, which was a horrible, oily salad she'd made. I
didn't comment on it because I knew Mother was
trying to encourage Rachel to cook. Not that this was
exactly cooking.

"Rachel," I said, "about Jeff and Phil . . ."

The phone rang. It was Mary El, telling me she
had a flat tire and I'd have to get to the theater some
other way. Damn! I'd wanted to talk to them about
Jeff and Phil. Well, later. When I got back to the
table Rachel was through eating.

"How could you be finished?"

"What do you mean, how? I am, that's all."

"You're a hog. You shouldn't eat so fast. It's not good
for you."

She got up from the table and put her dish in the
sink and started out of the kitchen.

"Where are you going? I want to talk to you."

"I have to take a shower."

"You took one this morning."

"So?" She looked at me like I was the world's filth-
iest person. Ever since she'd been seeing Kurt she'd
been showering constantly.

"I want to talk to you about something important,
Rachel."

"Not now," she said and left.

I rode to the theater with Rachel and her goony
friends. I wanted to tell them that we'd been wrong
to treat Phil and Jeff the way we had but, naturally,
we were being driven by one of the mothers, so there
was no way.

There was also no way to talk to anyone at the

theater. It was the final dress rehearsal and everyone was busy with makeup and costumes. Before the rehearsal started, Stimpson made an announcement.

"I'm afraid I have some bad news," she said. "The band has quit."

Everyone cheered. Stimpson smiled.

"Let me rephrase that. I have some good news . . . the band has quit."

Everyone cheered louder.

"They said they couldn't get it together so we'll just have a piano. Alan and Connie will divide up the songs."

"What about the trumpet in 'Blow, Gabriel'?" Maura asked.

"It happens," Stimpson said, "that Julia, our assistant stage manager, plays the trumpet. She'll do it from backstage."

More cheers.

"Okay," Stimpson said, "I'm not sure if we've got a good show or not—I'll let you know later. Let's go."

We made our entrances from the back of the theater through the audience, and as we were lining up I tapped Jeff on the shoulder.

"I'd like to talk with you, later," I said.

He just looked at me, nodded, and got into line.

When rehearsal was over Stimpson, as usual, gave us our notes. Then, just before dismissing us, she said:

"By the way: We have a good show!"

Everyone cheered and screamed and while that was going on I looked around for Jeff but I didn't see him.

I went downstairs and started taking off my makeup. Then I saw Jeff's reflection in my mirror as he passed by on his way to the boys' dressing room.

"Jeff," I said, standing in front of the curtain which separated the dressing rooms, "can I see you a minute?"

He came out.

"Can we go somewhere and talk?"

"Not tonight," he said.

I was shocked. "But I asked you earlier and you nodded."

"I wasn't thinking."

"It's very important that I talk to you tonight," I said.

"I just can't." He started back into the dressing room and I put my hand on his arm. He pulled away.

"I need to talk with you," I said.

"Camilla, I don't give a damn what you need. Your needs just don't interest me anymore. I've got other things on my mind besides you and your needs. Why don't you think about somebody else's needs for a change."

I started to tell him that that was exactly what I was trying to do, but he'd already disappeared. Well, this was really great! Here I was, ready to make up with Jeff, ready to tell him he could be what he wanted, and he didn't even care. As a matter of fact, nobody did. I'd tried a number of times with different people and nobody wanted to hear. Why was I knocking my brains out?

Who was I kidding? I hadn't tried very hard. I tried with Sam, knowing his mother would be there any second, and I tried with Rachel, knowing she was in a hurry. And now Jeff. But why should he come running just because I'd changed my mind? I'd given him a hard time like everyone else and if he didn't feel like talking to me when I wanted to . . . well, that was understandable. I'd talk to him tomorrow or the next day or the next.

As far as the other kids were concerned, well, everybody wanted to go home early and get a good night's sleep before the opening. It could wait. The truth of the matter was, and I only realized this when it was too late, I was *afraid* to talk to anyone about it because I knew what they'd say. They'd laugh at me, put me down, or maybe even accuse me of being queer. I just wasn't ready to be anything but a sheep.

Walt drove me home and wanted to come in, so I

let him. We played some James Taylor and Jethro Tull and had some Cokes. Then he wanted to make out (mostly out of boredom I think) but I didn't, so he sulked for a little while. For a change of pace I decided to try out my speech about Jeff and Phil.

"Walt," I said, "about Jeff and Phil . . ."

"How about that," he said.

I stared at him. I mean, that wasn't the kind of thing you said about something you'd known for a month.

"About Jeff and Phil," I said again, "I think it's awful . . ."

"It's the best thing that could've happened," he said.

Now I knew one of us was crazy. "What are you talking about?"

"Jeff and Phil," he said, looking at me like I was the crazy one. "What are you talking about?"

"What's the best thing that could have happened?"

"Don't you know?"

"Know what?" I could have wrung his skinny neck.

"It's over."

"It is? When? What happened?" No wonder Jeff didn't want to talk to me.

"I don't know the sordid details," he said, "but Phil is out with Penny tonight."

"Penny?"

"Yeah. Seems Penny's had a thing for him all along and she's been after him and after him and I guess she finally got him. She said she was gonna feed him tequila and make a man out of him tonight. Eben took bets that she couldn't do it, or rather that Phil couldn't. I guess we'll hear about it tomorrow."

I didn't know what to say. Or what to think. Penny? Why would Phil go off with Penny? If he was going to be straight—if he was going to be with a girl—why wasn't it me? And Jeff? He must be miserable.

"You mean Phil is really interested in Penny . . . really?"

"I don't know," he said and suddenly stood up. "I'd better get going."

"Walt, there's something you're not telling me."

"I gotta go." He walked to the door and I grabbed him.

"What's going on? What aren't you telling me?"

"I don't know what you're talking about. I told you what I know. I guess he digs girls, after all. Who knows? Who cares?"

"*I* care and your'e lying. Your nose is twitching. It always does that when you're lying."

"How do you know that?"

"Everybody knows it. Now tell me."

"Well . . . you know how Eben and Harlan and those guys have been on Phil's back. Anyway, something happened and Phil started screaming that being a fag was a choice—you know, he could be straight if he wanted to but he just didn't want to. So then Eben said he was a liar and bet Phil he couldn't make it with a girl, no matter what. Phil got all red in the face and started shaking and he kept screaming about a choice. So then Penny volunteered. That's all I know."

"Well, what did Jeff do? When did all this happen?"

"Before you got there tonight. Jeff told Phil he was letting them push him around—that he wasn't making a choice now—but Phil wouldn't listen. It was pretty hairy. Jeff said if Phil let those creeps force him into something like that, he couldn't respect him. Phil told Jeff to buzz off. That's it."

"And you mean, right now, Phil and Penny are . . . are . . . ?"

Walt shrugged.

I said good night to Walt and went up to bed. I couldn't believe what he'd told me, yet I knew it was the truth. His nose hadn't twitched once. Phil and Penny. It seemed impossible. First of all, as crazy as Penny was, I didn't think she'd do something like that. How desperate Phil must have felt to have agreed to it. In my heart of hearts, I knew he didn't care for

Penny . . . or me . . . or any girl. He just couldn't take the pressure. Sheep. Phil was a sheep, too.

The phone rang and I sat straight up in my bed. It was dark and I knocked over the lamp reaching for it. It kept ringing. Finally, I got to it.

"Camilla?"

It was Sam.

"What time is it?" I asked, yawning.

"It's . . . it's four thirty," he said. "Camilla . . . I . . . oh, God . . ."

I suddenly was wide awake. Sam sounded like he was crying. "What is it, Sam? Is it Linda?"

"No. Camilla," he said, his voice breaking over each syllable, "it's . . . Phil and Penny . . . they're dead."

Chapter 19

I don't think I ever wanted my mother more than when I hung up the phone. I got up to turn on a light and just stood there. *Phil and Penny . . . they're dead.* I kept hearing those five words over and over until they were scrambled in my mind and didn't make sense. I don't know how long I stood there, in the middle of the room, before I noticed that my legs were shaking. I sat down on the floor. I tried to think about what Sam had told me. It had happened on Route 25, on the big curve between Cutchogue and Peconic. Phil was driving. They went into a large tree. They weren't wearing seat belts and an empty quart of tequila was on the floor in the back. They were killed instantly. That was all. All. Over. The End. Curtain.

"What are you doin', Cam?" It was Rachel.

"Go back to bed."

"Why are you sittin' in the middle of the floor like that? Do you know what time it is?"

"Please, Rachel . . . go to bed." I didn't want to tell her.

"I heard the phone. Is somethin' wrong?"

I looked up at her, standing there in her yellow shortie nightgown. She looked very sweet . . . almost dear. She sat down on the floor facing me.

"You look horrible," she said. "Tell me what's wrong."

She looked very sincere and very concerned. I de-

197

cided to tell her. I opened my mouth but no words would come out. She put her hand on top of mine. It was hot and sweaty and I was glad it was there.

"Camel? Tell me. I *do* love you, you know."

"Oh, Rachel," I wailed. "It's Phil and Penny." And then I told her what I knew.

When I finished she moved next to me and put one of her small arms around my waist and took one of my hands in hers. She didn't say anything and I don't know how long we sat like that but when she finally spoke, light had started coming through the windows.

"Can't you cry?" she asked gently.

"No."

She nodded as though she understood and I think maybe she did . . . even if I didn't.

"I have to tell Jeff. Sam said no matter what's gone down between us this past month, I'm the only one who can tell him."

"Yes," Rachel said.

I looked at my clock. It was a quarter to six and the sun was rising over the bay. "I'd better get dressed."

Rachel nodded, squeezed my hand, and kissed me softly. We stood up and I found that I didn't know what to do next. Rachel handed me a pair of jeans and a shirt. Then she started unbuttoning my pajamas.

When she had finished dressing me she took me by the hand and led me downstairs.

"Would you like some orange juice?" she asked.

"No. I couldn't."

"Are you goin' to Jeff's now?"

"Yes."

"Would you like me to come with you?"

I shook my head and started for the door. Rachel opened it for me and I stepped out into the new day. A day Phil and Penny will never see, I thought. Once I was outside the screen door I couldn't move.

"Go on," Rachel said. "You can do it, Cam."

I put one foot in front of the other and started to walk. Then I stopped and turned around. Rachel was framed in the doorway like some kind of old-fashioned postcard. I wanted to thank her but I didn't have the strength. She raised her small hand in a wave and we both smiled miniature smiles as I turned away and headed toward Jeff's.

Jeff's house was silent as I stood on the doorstep. I knew if I knocked it wouldn't do any good but I hated to ring the bell. It was one of those awful chimes that played a tune. This one played "Ma-ry had a lit-tle lamb." But there was no other way. I pushed the button. How could anyone live with that? Only the D.L. would find that charming. I put my ear to the door but I didn't hear any stirrings. I had to ring the damn bell again. Oh, God, how could I tell Jeff? What could I say? What would he do? Maybe I should wait until later. I started to turn away from the door when it opened and there was Affectionate Al in his pajamas and robe. His hair was sticking straight up in two perfect horns.

"Yeah? What the hell do *you* want? Do you know what time it is?"

"I'm sorry, Mr. Grathwohl, but I have to speak to Jeff."

"Jeff? Are you crazy? It's six fifteen in the morning." He started to shut the door.

"Mr. Grathwohl, please, it's very important."

"Who is it, Albert?" I heard the D.L. somewhere behind him.

"What's so important that you have to talk now? You kids!"

"Who is it, Albert?" she squawked.

"Please," I said, "I know it's very early but this is really important."

The D.L. appeared at his elbow. "What do *you* want?"

"She says she has to talk to Jeff."

"Do you know what time it is?"

I wished they'd stop asking me that. "Yes, I know. I'm sorry . . . but I must talk to Jeff."

"Well that's just too bad," she said. "Jeffrey is in bed."

"Look, Mrs. Grathwohl, I wouldn't be here at this hour if it weren't something really important. Please let me speak to him."

"Oh, you kids," Mr. Grathwohl said, "the things you think are important. Wait . . . just wait until you get out in the real world and then you'll know what's important. Just wait."

"Close the door, Albert."

He started to close the door and I don't know what happened but I just opened my mouth and started to scream.

"Stop that . . . stop that," he said.

I kept screaming.

"She's gone crazy," the D.L. said.

I kept screaming.

"Will you stop that! You want the police here?"

"Then wake up Jeff," I said in a commanding voice.

"Close the door, Albert."

"If you do," I said, "I'll stand here and scream until I see Jeff or the police come."

"What's going on?" It was Jeff behind them.

"I have to talk to you, Jeff . . . now. It's very important."

"She's gone crazy, darling," the D.L. said to Jeff, grabbing his arm.

"I'm not kidding," I said. "You know I wouldn't be here if it weren't serious."

"Yeah," he said. He started to push through the screen door.

"Where are you going?" the D.L. asked, still holding on to him.

"Let go," he said.

"You can't go out like that, you're in your pajamas. What will the neighbors think?"

"I'm your neighbor," I said.

"You shut up, you little tramp."

"Let go, Mother." He wrenched his arm free and came outside. "C'mon."

We started walking down the beach.

"Where are you going, Jeffrey?" the D.L. was screaming.

"Ah, they're all crazy. Come back to bed, Eleanor."

Jeff and I kept walking until we couldn't hear them anymore and then we stopped.

"What is it?" he asked.

Just like that. What is it? What could I say? I have some bad news? Something terrible has happened? Lead up to it slowly . . . but how? I'd never had to tell anyone that someone he loved was dead. There is no easy way, is there?

"What is it?" he asked again.

I stared at him. At this moment he was confused and perhaps hurt by what Phil had said he was going to do. But he wasn't wiped out. In a second, with three words, I would wipe him out. In one second, everything would change for Jeff. How could I do that to him? But if I didn't do it now, someone else would do it later.

"Did you wake up my whole house just so you could stand here and stare at me? Huh?"

"Something's happened," I finally murmured.

"What?"

"I . . . I . . ."

"Come on . . . how bad could it be?"

"It's *very* bad," I said. This was no good. I was torturing him. Why couldn't I just say it? Three words, that's all. Say it.

"Well, what is it?"

"I don't know how to tell you."

He looked deep into my eyes. "Camilla," he said, softly.

I think he knew then but I'll never be sure. There could be no more stalling . . . no hesitation. This was the moment.

"Phil is dead."

He didn't say anything, at least not with words. He made a small sound, as though someone had punched him in the stomach. We stood there staring at one another, sea gulls calling overhead. The sun was beginning to feel hot.

"How?" he asked.

I told him what I knew.

"Maybe it's a mistake," he said. "How did Sam know?"

"His father's a volunteer fireman." On the North Fork, when there's a serious accident, the volunteer fire department is called out.

"Maybe his father made a mistake."

I didn't say anything because we both knew there had been no mistake. Then he turned and looked out at the bay.

"It's a beautiful blue today, isn't it?" he said.

"Yes."

He was silent a moment and then he whirled around and grabbed me by the shoulders. "You killed him," he yelled. "All of you . . . you all killed him. I hate you . . . I hate you . . . I wish you were *all* dead."

Then he started running down the beach, his robe open now and flapping around his body. I ran after him. Not to catch up but just so he wouldn't really be alone. Eventually, he stopped running and started to walk. I did the same, staying a good distance behind him. It must have been at least forty minutes before he stopped and slumped to the ground. I stopped where I was and sat down to wait. As the sound of his sobbing floated down to me, my own tears finally came.

Chapter 20

~~~~~~~~~~~~~~~~~~~~~~~~~~~~~~~~

Eventually, Jeff stopped crying, or at least the sound stopped. There were still tears in his eyes when he walked over to me. I stood up.

"What are you doing here? What do you want?"

"I want to help you. I want to be your friend."

"You're a little late, aren't you?" He started walking toward home.

"Please, Jeff . . . I'm so sorry . . . don't you know . . . don't you know how sorry I am?" I fell into step beside him.

"So what?"

And he was right. So what? What difference did it make if I was sorry? It wouldn't bring Phil back—or Penny. And it wouldn't change what had been done to Phil, what had driven him to go with Penny and get drunk and ram into a tree. We walked along slowly, saying nothing. Jeff kicked the sand as he walked.

"It just isn't fair," he mumbled. "It isn't fair. Phil never did anything to anybody. All he did was love me. I still don't see how that hurt anybody else."

"He couldn't take the pressure," I said.

"I'm not speaking to you."

I wanted to tell him that the reason I'd wanted to talk to him last night was because I was sorry—because I finally knew what I'd been doing was wrong. But I also knew that right now *I* wasn't the issue.

There would be time later to work things out with Jeff.

"What are you going to do?" I asked.

"Do? What do you mean, do?"

"I don't know exactly."

"I think I'll go visit my cousin in New York. I think I should get away from here."

"When?"

"Today—right now—as soon as I get back to the house I'll call him."

I hesitated before I spoke, but not for long. "But Jeff, what about the show?"

He looked at me coldly. "What about it?"

"We open tonight."

"*You* open tonight."

"What do you mean?"

"Just what I said. *You* open tonight, not me."

"But Jeff . . ."

"Listen, Camilla, if you think I'm going to be in that crummy show after everything that's happened, you're mistaken."

"But who'll do your part?"

"I don't give a damn."

I knew how he felt. God knows, I didn't feel like opening a show and he must have felt even less like it. I knew the show could open—Lillian could take Penny's place and we'd do without a prompter— but there was no one to replace Jeff. Mr. Whitney wasn't a major role but it was important. There was no way to cut the part.

"We can't cut the part," I said.

"I told you . . . I don't care what you do with it."

"Jeff, we won't be able to do the show if . . ."

"So don't do it."

"Don't you think . . . I mean, sixty kids have worked hard for six weeks. You can't let them all down like that—you . . ."

He stopped walking and turned toward me, his eyes narrowed. "The hell I can't! What have they done for me lately, huh? Why should I do anything for them when all they've done is put me down, torture me, and drive Phil so crazy he killed himself. 'Cause that's what happened, you know. I don't care what anyone calls it—drunken driving . . . an accident—I know the truth, and so do you."

"Yes, I know," I said.

"Okay. Then you tell me . . . you find me one good reason why I should do anything for any of you. Find me the reason and I'll do it."

I couldn't, of course. He owed us nothing. The rest of the way home we were silent.

When we got back to our beach it was about eight o'clock and I watched Jeff walk to his house without saying another word. I knew I should call Sam and the others but I didn't feel like it quite yet. I should also be getting ready for work. But, of course, I wasn't going to work, was I? I kept forgetting: Two of my friends had died. Died. Dead. Death. When my father died I was only a little child and I hardly knew him and all I understood was that I wouldn't be seeing him again. As I grew older, I remembered him less and less and what I missed was the idea of a father, not the actual man. When my dog Jeep was run over by a car I don't remember if I cried or not but I do remember calling everyone on the phone to tell them. Jeep died, I'd said, almost happily. I guess I wanted sympathy—I knew that's what people got when someone they loved died. And that had been it. I still had all my grandparents and no one else I'd known had died. Now two of them. I would never see them again. Never. I couldn't imagine how long never was. I would never again see Penny's big round eyes dancing with some mischievous idea, or see Phil smile or hear him laugh or . . . or anything. How could it be possible? I felt the tears starting again. Was it true what I'd heard Mother say—you cry for yourself, *your* loss, not for the dead? Probably. What was the difference?

There was a touch on my shoulder. "Darling?" It was Mother.

"What are you doing here?" She wasn't expected back until tonight—in time for the opening.

"Rachel called me when you went to Jeff's. I know everything. Why haven't you talked to me? No, never mind, that isn't important now. I want to help you, I'm with you . . . do you understand?"

I nodded and then I flung my arms around her neck and cried, loud and long. There is just no one else like a mother at certain times in life, and I'd never been so grateful for mine as I was that morning.

Ray had driven up from the city with Mother and when we walked into the house he was standing in the kitchen, a glass of orange juice in each hand.

"You've got to have something," he said. "It's going to be a long, hard day and night."

We each took a glass. He put his arm around me and kissed me. "I'm sorry," he said.

I nodded. Ray poured coffee for all of us and we sat down at the kitchen table. I began to talk, nonstop, telling them every detail of what had happened since the Fourth of July. They nodded and made an occasional comment, but neither of them interrupted. When I finished—ending with Jeff's refusal to be in the show—I took a deep breath and said I was hungry. Ray said he would make me some eggs.

"Is it awful for me to eat?" I asked.

"Of course not, what do you mean?"

"I mean, here I am eating, and Phil and . . ."

"You're alive, Cam," Mother said.

"But in the movies and books and things, people don't eat for weeks when they're grieving."

"Everyone grieves . . . mourns in a different way," Mother said.

"Just like everyone loves in a different way," Ray added. "When I was about your age I found out that my brother was a homosexual. It was years before I could look him straight in the eye or shake his hand with any conviction. I was terribly ashamed of him. But when I got older, I realized that homosexuality was his way and heterosexuality was my way. It didn't matter who he loved or what he did in bed. He was a nice, bright guy and I liked him and that was really all that mattered."

"I guess I'll be running into it a lot if I'm going to be an actress," I said.

"That may be," Ray said; "but I'm not talking about my brother who's the director, by the way. I'm talking about another brother. He's a lawyer."

"I don't understand why we all acted that way. And if it's not wrong, well, why does everyone put it down?" I asked.

"Because we're all afraid of things we don't understand," Mother said. "Homosexuality—and that includes lesbianism—has been part of life as long as there have been people and it always will be. I don't think anybody quite understands why some people are and some aren't. There are several schools of thought: Some think it's environment, others think it's biological, still others think it's a choice. The uninformed and the ignorant think it's evil or even a disease."

"What do *you* think?" I asked.

"I'm not sure. Homosexuality and alcoholism are the two things that the medical and psychiatric professions know very little about. But I do know this . . . as long as you don't hurt anyone else, you have a right to be what you want to be."

"Do you think we killed Phil?"

"I understand what Jeff means," Ray said. "There's no doubt that what you kids did was terrible . . . rotten. But it didn't cause Jeff to go off the deep end. Phil, obviously, was less stable. Unless he'd made peace with himself—unless he'd gotten help—it probably would have happened sooner or later. I'm not excusing anybody though."

"I was a coward, wasn't I?"

Mother stroked my hair. "A bit," she said; "but

you can't live with regrets—there's no point in that. What you can do is act on what you've learned. Give people room . . . let them be."

"Thank you for coming home early," I said. "I'd better call the kids now."

As we made up for opening night, a lot of kids were crying and the makeup kept running. It was terribly quiet, not like an opening night at all—except, of course, for Eben, who was dashing around behaving like nothing at all had happened. I think everyone knew then that something definitely was wrong with him. We ignored him and when he said something like, what the hell, there was one less faggot in the world, even Harlan was disgusted. I guess not everybody learns from something like this.

Stimpson had arranged for Mike, the stage manager, to walk through Jeff's part with the book. We all knew it would be awful because Mike had trouble reading, but there just wasn't anyone else. She'd said we could cancel the performance if we wanted and that the community would understand, but we voted unanimously to go on. I think we knew if we canceled we would have to face each other and ourselves and we weren't quite ready to. There was going to be plenty of time for that.

Then, fifteen minutes before curtain, Jeff showed up. No one said anything while he got into his costume and put on his makeup. As we stood quietly in line on the stairs, waiting for the signal to go up, Jeff cleared his throat and spoke.

"I just want you to know," he said, "I'm not doing this because I feel I owe you anything. I'm doing it because I don't believe in an eye for an eye, that's all."

Eben opened his mouth to say something but Sam gave him an elbow in the stomach. Then the signal came and we heard the overture begin.

It wasn't the best of the eight performances that we gave, but it wasn't bad. During the curtain call a lot of us stood there singing "Anything Goes" with tears running down our faces. We heard later that most of the audience thought it was adorable that we'd cried over the show.

There was no cast party that night, and two days later we went to the funerals. Phil's was at eleven in the morning and Penny's was at one that afternoon. Everyone but Eben and Bruce came to Phil's funeral.

I had never been to a funeral before but I'd seen them in movies and on television so I knew pretty much what to expect. Mother was there but she said she didn't expect Rachel or me to sit with her. All the kids sat together in our various groups. None of us had been asked to be pallbearers because the Chrysties really didn't know any of us. I'd asked Jeff if he wanted me to sit with him but he said he'd rather sit alone. He looked awful. I don't think he'd slept since it happened and he was thinner than I'd ever seen him.

The casket was, of course, at the front of the church. And it was open. I was surprised about that because I had heard all kinds of rumors that both of them had been terribly disfigured.

Mr. and Mrs. Chrystie and Phil's brother sat in front on the right-hand side. There were two much older people next to them and I assumed they were Phil's grandparents. They were both crying a lot but not as much as Mrs. Chrystie. Or at least not as loud. Mr. Chrystie didn't seem to be crying at all. I remembered what Phil had told me about his father not liking him too much and I wondered if he wasn't crying because he didn't care or because he was doing the old male thing of being a stoic. I decided it was the second.

Then the hymns stopped and the eulogy began. I have to confess I really didn't hear a word of it. Oh, maybe a word here and there, but I wasn't actually listening. My mind was on the casket. It wasn't that I was afraid . . . I don't think. I mean what's to be afraid of? When people are dead they're dead. They can't

hurt you. And yet it *was* fear I was feeling. There
was no mistaking that crawly dampness on the back of
my neck or the heavy pounding my heart was doing.
It may have been my first experience with death
but it certainly wasn't my first with fear. I couldn't
figure out what was making me feel that way until
I noticed that people were getting up and going to
the casket. Then I knew. It was simply the thought of
looking at Phil. Here I was, sixteen years old, and I
had never seen a dead person. What if I fainted? Or
threw up or something? But that was silly—why
should that happen? What was it about looking at
dead people that might make you do that? They
were just lying there like they were sleeping, weren't
they?

"Camilla?"

I felt a tug at my arm. It was Janet who was sitting
next to me.

"C'mon . . . we have to go look at Phil."

"Why?" I asked.

"Because we have to," Mary El said, leaning across
Janet. "Move."

I was on the aisle. "Why do we *have* to?"

"Oh, don't start," Janet said. "If you're not going
to look, at least move so we can go up."

So that's what I did. I stood up and stepped out
into the aisle and let them go past.

"Gross," Mary El whispered as she passed me.

Was it? Or was it gross to go and stare at him? I
really didn't know. I stood in the aisle a few seconds,
watching the people file past the casket, and then I
decided that to make a decision about it I had to go
up. There would be lots more funerals in my lifetime
and if I was going to have a point of view about them,
I should experience at least one the way everybody
else did.

Slowly I walked down the aisle. When I got to the
casket I stopped, took two more steps, and looked in.
As I had expected, his eyes were closed and his hands
were folded across his chest. I had seen enough

movies to know that would be his position. But movies are one thing, and real life . . . real death is another. There was rouge on his cheeks and his lips were colored and he looked like he was made of wax. It was awful. That body lying there in the blue-lined coffin was no more Phil than I was. I turned away quickly and started back up the aisle. Before I had even gotten to my seat I had made my decision. Never, never again would I look at a dead person if I had a choice. There was no point. It certainly did nothing for the person who was dead and served no purpose for the person who was looking, as far as I could figure. It was just some terrible old custom that people followed without thinking about it. I made up my mind right there and then to leave instructions that I was to have a closed casket. *I was to have a closed casket.* The words bounced around my head like a tennis ball gone wild. Someday *I* was going to die. It was the first time I had ever *really* thought about my own death.

Not that up until this point I had thought I was immortal or anything. It was just that I hadn't thought about it at all. But now, sitting in this church with Phil lying in his casket, there was no way I couldn't think about it. If it could happen to him and Penny so suddenly, it could happen to me. It was a terrible thought and one I wanted to push aside. I guess that's called not facing reality. And the reality was that even if I didn't die suddenly or die young, someday I *was* going to die. I began to feel like I couldn't breathe. I knew from listening to my mother talk about patients with other analysts that I was having an anxiety attack. I guess knowing that helped a bit because soon my breathing was okay.

Okay, I said to myself, so someday I was going to die. I was no different from anyone else in that regard. There was no reason to dwell on it, make myself sick about it. It was a fact that there was nothing I could do about it. The important thing was to live . . . and to live the best way I knew how. I couldn't do anything about my death but I could do something about my life, and that's what I would concentrate on: getting the most out of life that I possibly could without hurting anyone else's life. I felt better.

Everyone was rising. The pallbearers were picking up the casket and leaving the church. Phil's family followed the casket out and then we all left.

The service at the cemetery was short. The minister said a prayer and then the casket was lowered into the grave. Everybody cried a lot, including me, and then it was over. We all got back into our cars and headed for the church where Penny's funeral was being held.

Hers was altogether different from Phil's. While his was what you might call traditional, Penny's was kind of offbeat. For instance, at Phil's they played hymns and at Penny's they had a friend of the Lademans' playing the score from *Jesus Christ Superstar*, which was some of Penny's favorite music. A lot of older people were commenting on it, saying it was shocking and dreadful and stuff like that, but I thought it was neat. I mean, what did hymns have to do with Penny? The second thing that was different was that Penny's casket was closed. I thought it was because the rumors I had heard were true but later I learned that the Lademans didn't believe in open caskets. The third thing that was different was the service. Byron Krausse, the minister, was very different from any other minister on the North Fork. He was very young and he had a full reddish beard. He started the service by saying that he didn't know Penny too well and rather than say a lot of ordinary things about her it was his wish, as well as her family's, to have anyone who wanted to, come up and say something about Penny. There was a lot of buzzing and clucking of tongues from some of the older people, and then I saw Sam walking up to the front. He cleared his throat and pushed his hair out of his eyes.

"Once when Penny and I were walking on the beach we found a sea gull with a broken leg. Penny took the sea gull home and put a splint on his leg and took care of him for a whole month. When he was better she let him go. She cried for a whole day because she'd grown to love that bird, whom she called Joshua. I probably would have kept him but Penny thought more about the bird's feelings than her own. That's the way she was."

Then Sam went back to his seat. Janet went up next.

Her voice cracked slightly as she began to talk. "Whenever I was depressed Penny could make me laugh. She always had a funny story to tell and, if she knew you were upset, even when she was herself, she concentrated on making *you* laugh."

One by one the kids went up. I was really surprised when Maura walked to the front.

"I didn't know Penny too well but, well, she very much wanted the part of Reno Sweeney that I got this summer. For a long time I thought she hated me, and maybe she did, but about two weeks ago she came up to me after a rehearsal and said: 'Maura, I gotta tell ya . . . you're really good. I'm not sure I could've done it.' That meant more to me than if the biggest producer on Broadway had said I was good. And all I could think was that if things had been reversed I don't know if I would have had the guts to say it to her. I think she was a super person."

By now everyone was crying. None of us had known that Penny had said that to Maura and it showed us a side of her we hadn't known.

Finally, I went up. "After listening to everything that everyone else has said I'm really sorry I didn't know Penny a lot better. What I knew I liked but it makes me realize that there's a whole lot more to people than we know. Penny made me laugh too and sometimes she made me mad and sometimes I just didn't know what to make of her, but basically I think she was a good person and made the most of her life and that's what most important. I'll miss her a lot."

There were three or four people after me and then Byron Krausse said a short prayer. When that was over the pallbearers, who consisted of Sam, Walt, Eben, Penny's brother, and two men, led the procession out of the church.

After the service at the cemetery we all went to the Sweet Shop. All except Jeff, who went home I guess. We all agreed that when we died we wanted to have a funeral like Penny's. Sam said he wanted to be cremated and Walt said he wanted to be frozen. Mary El said she couldn't stand to think about it and couldn't we talk about something else.

"You can talk all you want about something else," Janet said, "but it's going to happen to you too someday. This we know."

"Well, it's gross to go on and on about it."

"No it isn't. It's dumb not to face it," I said.

"You face it if you want to, Camilla. I'm going to put it out of my mind."

"Are you going to put Phil and Penny out of your mind, too?"

"Well, no, but I'm not going to dwell on them either," Mary El said.

"I, for one," Janet said, "will never forget them."

"I didn't mean I'd forget them. I just mean I don't want to dwell on them forever. I don't see what good it'll do anybody to keep thinking . . ."

I interrupted. "You don't want to face that they're dead. Well, the fact is that they are. We're never going to see either of them again and we can't run away from that."

Nobody said anything then and one by one we made excuses and left for our various destinations. I went home and stayed in my room for the rest of the afternoon, listening to music and thinking about Penny and Phil and the pleasure each of them had given me. I guess you could say it was my own memorial. That night I went off to do the show.

The performances got better and better, and by closing night we were terrific. We even had a final party. But behind and underneath everything, we were a sorry bunch of kids and when it was all over we were glad to get away from each other . . . because no matter whose eyes you looked into, you were reminded. I think that year, for the first time in our lives, we were really glad when school began—glad to be starting something new and to be able to put that awful summer behind us.

Chapter 21

So now it's October and Janet and Mary El and I are getting together this afternoon with some other kids to plan the decorations for the Halloween dance.

A lot has happened in the last two months. Tina, naturally, broke up with Eben because she's a decent, lovely person and after everything that happened she couldn't stomach him anymore. Walt went off to college and writes that he's met a very nice girl. I'm glad because he and I were never right for each other.

Sam has finally gotten over Linda—she married Burt in September—and, believe it or not, he suddenly realized it was Mary El he loved all the time. Needless to say, Mary El is in heaven.

Janet has lost fourteen more pounds, stopped smoking, and has a crush on the new science teacher.

Rachel broke up with Kurt and, once again, goes for weeks on end without showering, but I don't bug her about it anymore. She's a good kid in spite of it.

My mother and Ray are getting married over Thanksgiving weekend. I'm going to be maid of honor and Ray's lawyer brother will be best man. Ray's going to sell his house in Stonington and come to live with us.

Jeff and I made up and yesterday he wrote to me that he's met someone he likes a lot. He says that the boy, Richard, will never take Phil's place . . . but then, no one should ever take anyone's place. He thinks they'll have a nice relationship and he's planning to bring him home for Thanksgiving. I look forward to meeting him, as I told Jeff when I answered his letter last night.

And me? Well, I have the lead in *Leave it to Jane*, the play we're doing in school, and I've sent away for my applications to Carnegie-Mellon and Julliard—I'm still going to be an actress—and, after the Halloween decoration meeting, I'm going down to the Southold Sweet Shop and meet Jim Harris. Jim has changed a lot since the summer and doesn't hang around with Bruce and Harlan or any of those guys any more. He says I'm a beautiful person and maybe if we go out together often enough, some of it might rub off on him. I'm certainly willing to give it a try.

ABOUT THE AUTHOR

SANDRA SCOPPETTONE's plays have been staged on television and off-off-Broadway. Her play, *Stuck*, was one of twelve dramas by new playwrights performed in 1972 at the Eugene O'Neill Theatre Center in Waterford, Connecticut, and she has received a grant from the Ludwig Vogelstein Foundation to write a play about George Sand. Sandra Scoppettone grew up in South Orange, New Jersey, and now lives in Southold, New York. Although this is her first novel for young readers, she is the author (with Louise Fitzhugh) of two picture books, *Suzuki Beane* and *Bang Bang You're Dead*.